by

melissa marr

writing as
Ronnie Douglas

"A full-throttle read that's dangerously sexy and exciting. I can't wait to see what happens next!" —Jeaniene Frost, NYT best-selling author of the Night Huntress series, on *Unlawful*

"The hero, oh the hero, steals the show here. Adam is hot, hot, hot and readers will want him as badly as Sasha does." —RT Magazine

"Douglas opens her Knights in Black Leather series with this satisfyingly angsty new adult contemporary...Douglas's characters are terrific."--Publishers Weekly on *Undaunted*

"A gripping new series with enough tension and heart to keep the reader rapidly flipping pages."--Jay Crownover, New York Times bestselling author, on *Undaunted*

"Douglas has penned a steamy romance sure to please...Fans of the motorcycle club genre will be eager for more." --RT Book Reviews on *Undaunted*

"Douglas has pulled from several hot tropes to craft an engaging, quick read that brings top-notch chemistry to each page."--HeroesandHearbreakers.com on *Undaunted*

"Douglas (a pseudonym for bestselling author Melissa Marr) serves up healthy portions of both heat and sweet." --*Publisher's Weekly* on *Unruly*

PRAISE FOR THE WICKED LOVELY SERIES (MELISSA MARR):

"Marr offers readers a fully imagined faery world that runs alongside an everyday world, which even non-fantasy (or faerie) lovers will want to delve into" --*Publisher's Weekly* (starred review)

"Fans of the fey world will devour this sequel to Wicked Lovely. Marr has created a world both harsh and lush, at once urban and natural." --*School Library Journal*

"Marr has done it again with this dark, beautifully woven story of love, magic, and belonging." --*Romantic Times Bookclub*

"Complex and involving." -*New York Times Book Review*

SUGAR

S inners Ink was the sort of place that could be any tattoo shop. Even from the parking lot, I could see the racks of flash art that jutted out from the walls in mounted poster frames, and other available images were in flat frames covering a lot of the open space. Interspersed among the available tattoos were several magazine covers that highlighted either an artist who currently worked at SI or one who used to work there. Tattooists were often a transient lot, doing stints at shops while they traveled.

What set this shop apart was one artist.

Or maybe that was my hormones talking.

I sat on the hood of my sedan in the shade of the building. The car wasn't going to win any awards for looks, but it got me to and from work and wherever else I needed to get in Rio Verde. I settled for that. Honestly, I settled for a lot of things the past few years. Now, I was trying to think bigger, to let myself dream of a future, of happiness.

The roar of a Harley made my gaze lift and my pulse flutter. I wasn't a motorcycle junkie, just a little more than excited by seeing the man on this bike. The bike was worth a look: classic with a silver dragon detailed on the body. The man was worth more looks—and I was definitely looking. I'd been looking even when I wasn't admitting it to myself, but I was single now.

The bike's engine cut off, and Adam smiled at me.

"Hey, Sasha."

Adam Bradbery was six feet of taut muscle and gorgeous ink. With his shoulder-length hair and five o'clock shadow, he looked like the kind of guy who had nothing but bad habits, but he was actually a health nut—unlike his cousin, Tommy. My ex. He was the reason I even knew Adam.

"Am I late?" Adam said as he climbed off his bike.

"No. I'm early." I didn't add that I was early because I liked watching him ride up to the shop.

He nodded, eying the coffee cup beside me on the hood of my car.

"I brought coffee for you." I slid off the hood and onto the ground where I was reminded of exactly how short I was. Next to him, I looked like a child.

"You didn't have to bring this, Sash."

"No big deal, Adam." I shrugged, as if my lie would be more believable for it. Fresh ground beans. Fresh brew. Based my schedule around when it would be ready, so it was still warm.

I held out the cup.

He took it, sniffed, and tasted. After a sigh that sent my mind right back to places it ought not be, he said, "Perfect."

What I wouldn't give to have him sigh like that after—

I snapped that mental door shut. We were friends. Friends was exactly what I needed, especially from him.

Adam had rolled into town a couple of years ago to check on Tommy, and then he'd stayed. Several of the framed magazine covers inside the shop were his. Many of the customers buying small impulse tattoos were because of him, too. More than a few women were willing to pay to have his hands on them.

I wasn't any better than them.

I tried to tell myself I wasn't like them, but being his friend didn't change the fact that I wanted the man naked.

He unlocked the shop and ushered me inside before heading over to the alarm. Tattoos are often a cash business here, so the shop was a target.

I walked further inside with the comfort of a person who spent more than a few hours here. Honestly, I was more comfortable like this: just us. When the shop was open, Adam was different. He had to be. He smiled more, made people at ease with a friendly voice, answering the same questions as if they weren't things easily found on the shop website or by asking, Betsey, the woman at the front desk. They wanted him to answer, though.

To connect.

To have his attention for that one moment.

When the shop was closed, I had all of his attention—especially now that I was here on my own. At first, back when I was dating Tommy, I had to share Adam. I felt like a shit for admitting that back then. What kind of person was I if I was making eyes at my man's cousin?

But Tommy and me were like two poisons trying to see which of us was worse.

"You okay?" Adam was back, and I'd been lost enough in my thoughts not to hear him.

"Thinking about Tommy."

Adam misunderstood. "You're both better off this way."

I nodded. He was right. Everyone who'd told me that exact thing was right, and I wasn't arguing with them. Not now. Tommy liked drugs more than he'd liked me, and when we were together, I was right there with him. High and stupid. It hadn't even occurred to me that I might deserve better.

Not then.

"Let's see where we are," Adam said, sounding like he had

countless times since I'd arrived at the shop crying and bruised a few months ago. He put me back together.

And I was going to stay that way.

"Sit," he said softly, motioning to the black padded table where I'd stretched out on my stomach and on my back to have him tattoo me.

I sat like a patient in front of a doctor, but I wasn't feeling like a patient.

"How's it feel?" He stood close to me, leaned back so his arm brushed my shoulder as he reached back.

I started to say I would move, turn or lay down on the table or . . .

But then Adam lifted the edge of my shirt, baring my back. His fingertips glided over my skin and left a ripple of longing everywhere he touched.

I reminded myself that this was business. I was just another woman who had paid him to draw on my skin. I was no one special.

"Looking good," he said.

The tattoo. I reminded myself that he was an artist, looking at a piece of canvas he'd decorated. I was just the one wearing the canvas. I still sounded shaky when I said, "I have been careful. Lots of water. Rest. Doing all the things you said."

Adam straightened, still too close for comfort, and said, "You know those things are about being healthy in general, not just for the tattoo, right?"

He gave my shoulder a gentle push, and I all but flopped onto my back in eagerness. On my back, Adam looking down at me, yeah, I had a few dreams that started like this.

"So let's do a bit more today," he suggested, looking down at my side where the last tattoo session had ended.

"More. Right. More is good." I had, apparently, lost the power of coherent speech.

He smiled. "You look happy."

I couldn't answer. I was. He made me feel powerful and beautiful.

"Why don't you stay there while I set up?" His voice sounded deeper to me then.

"You're probably busy and—"

"Stay there," he repeated.

And I found myself nodding. He wasn't being pushy or mean, just reassuring me, and honestly, I liked it when he was pushy. I worried about that tendency, about how much I liked being told what to do. I wondered at first if it was why I couldn't stop fantasizing about Adam. He looked intimidating even in his gentlest moods. He had the sheer size that meant that he didn't need to raise a fist to stop a fight. He was all muscle, and his spa-perfect skin was liberally decorated with tattoos.

It wasn't just the way he looked, though. It was the fact that he was gentle, that he was a good man.

I stayed still as he prepared the tattoo machine and the inks.

Adam wasn't just attentive to his body; he was concerned about other people's health, too. So he took the time to make sure that each customer was safe. Autoclave. New needles. Fresh ink. Gloves. There was as little of a contamination risk as possible when someone was on his table.

Finally, he was ready. The machine gave a few hums as he adjusted speed and checked everything.

Then he looked at me, and I realized that I'd been staring at him the whole time.

"Do you want to take that off?"

I sat up and pulled my shirt off, leaving me sitting in front of Adam in jeans and a blue bra. Not exactly what friends did, but he saw plenty of people's skin. It was his job. I was just another body on the table. That was all.

But the heat in his eyes said something else, something I

couldn't let myself believe. He looked at me like . . . well . . . like I imagined he looked at all the other girls he slept with. I needed to remember them. I was just another girl, one he treated different because I didn't fall into his bed.

I stretched out on the table again.

He didn't look at my face as he carefully swiped my skin with a cleanser.

For several moments, he studied me, his eyes following the lines of my body, and then he met my eyes and asked, "Are you ready?"

It felt like a question that was bigger than tattooing.

"Just along my ribs." I felt like I whispered it, but my mouth was too dry.

He slid closer and rested his arm on me, forearm over my hip. He'd done this last time, too. It made sense because of where he was tattooing—but to me it felt sexual.

His breath warmed my bare skin.

Then he turned on the machine again.

The vibrations reverberated through his arm, more so when he started working.

Absently, he moved closer.

I tensed.

"Is this okay, Sasha?"

Mutely, I nodded.

"Do you want me to move my arm?" He stared at me, his expression innocent. "Are you comfortable?"

"I like it where it is," I admitted shakily.

"You sure?"

"Keep going," I said. "I trust you."

Adam smiled then. "I want you to be happy. If there's anything—"

"Tattoo me."

And he did. There was no way he didn't notice my breathing,

the way I was tensing. I didn't move though, didn't arch my hips into him when he paused the machine to dip it in more ink. I whimpered, and not from pain.

"Some people like tattooing. The process, I mean," he said mildly.

"I can see that," I managed.

"Oh?"

I closed my eyes. "Beautiful man, bare skin, and those vib . . . vibrations."

He chuckled. "So it's like that, Sasha?"

I bit my lip as he resumed silence. His hands were on me, and my body was screaming for release.

Then he stopped. Just stopped. "More?"

I blinked at him.

"How far are we going today?" he asked softly.

For a moment, I wondered what he was offering because I wanted to go further, to never stop. My entire reserve of self-control was focused on not lifting my hips or moaning.

He sat up, and I felt lost, desperate for more. Then my brain forced a smidge of focus on me. This was just a job to him. I was reacting like it was personal. Either that, or I was treating him like an orgasm for hire.

"I gotta go." I sat up so fast I felt dizzy, grabbed my shirt and headed toward the door without having it on.

I flicked the lock and shoved my way into the light. The shop alarm was still blaring behind me when I slid into the car and fled.

I wasn't like this. I was his friend. That was it. And I wasn't about to turn a tattoo into some sort of budget orgasm. Friends don't use friends, and I wasn't going to use Adam.

SUGAR

I won't say I avoided Adam the next two weeks, but I will say that I arrived at work exactly on time. If there was a chance to catch me, he wasn't going to find it. I felt like a skank, not that there was a thing in the world wrong with a sex drive. I owned mine, and woe to anyone who tried to make me feel guilt for the exact same urges that men were allowed to celebrate. No, what I felt guilty about was the fact that I'd come near to embarrassing myself. Adam didn't deserve to be treated like a walking sex toy. He was a friend, and I'd been unfair to him. To both of us.

"Hey! Sugar," Lanie, one of the girls who filled in at the shop when Rio Verde was filled with co-eds, stood in the middle of the mostly empty shop.

"Mila called out again?" My best friend and co-worker wasn't so great with being at the store regularly. She got "itchy feet," as she called them. She might not totally take off, but she would go on short rambles—which she called "the flu" when talking to our boss but were really camping trips up toward the Grand Canyon or Flagstaff area usually.

"She's tired from having that flu," Lanie said sadly. "She'll be in tonight though."

"Right." I nodded as if I believed this, although clearly it wasn't true. Anyone who really knew Mila knew she went off on her own, and the "flu" she was recovering from was being tired from hiking or kayaking or some other action-packed weekend.

Ian looked up from the guitar he was tuning. "She ought to take a few days off to rest the way she gets sick."

Ian and I exchanged a smile. He was on and off again with Mila in a friends-with benefits way, and I sometimes thought that he was only with her because he thought someone ought to be keeping an eye on her. He wasn't wrong.

"Maybe you can go take her soup," I teased.

He nodded. "I'll tell her it was your idea."

I held up both hands in front of me. I wasn't looking for trouble with Mila. She was the closest thing to family I'd had—aside from Tommy. She stood by me when Tommy and I made up over and over. She pointed out that I was idiot, of course, but she still stayed in my life. The only other person I knew that I could trust was Adam.

My brain flashed back to being stretched out in front of him. Topless. Excited.

I shook my head and looked around the coffee shop. It was still pretty dead, and I wasn't sure we needed Mila tonight. We certainly wouldn't need her *and* Lainie. Even on a weekend, we weren't likely to be packed now that the college kids were all headed home for the summer. Weirdly, no one seemed to want to stay in our inevitably burning hot, 120-degree summer weather. As soon as the semester ended, they all started to take off for cooler states.

Ian strummed his guitar, killing time at the shop. Sometimes I thought he got bored at home because he spent a lot of time here. Maybe he was just more into Mila than I realized.

~

By evening, the shop was still barely full. By night, Mila and I were the only two people still working. Laine was gone. Ian was playing for the stragglers.

And I was exhaling a sigh of relief that Adam hadn't come in. Two weeks now, and I was still successfully dodging him.

"Red alert," Mila murmured. "I'm going to see if Ian needs anything."

I looked up to see Adam walk in the door just as Mila abandoned me at the front counter.

There he stood, tall beautiful and smiling at me.

"Hey." I sounded lame. What was the right word for *oh-shit-you're-here?*

"I'm starting to think you're avoiding me, Sasha." Adam raised his voice to be heard over Ian's singing.

"I've just been taking time to myself." I knew I sounded about as honest as I really was.

"You don't like the ink?"

"I do!"

He nodded. "So you don't like me tattooing you?"

I sighed. "Obviously, that's not it."

He smiled then. "Then we'll schedule again."

I floundered, trying to figure out what to do to avoid this. "Kona!" I held up a hand. "Let me get you a cup."

"You always know what I need," he said in that damned sexy voice.

"I pay attention." I closed my eyes as soon as I said it. I *wasn't* flirting. I was trying my damnedest not to do that with him. I was pretty sure that I was the only woman in Rio Verde who tried *not* to flirt with him.

"Not quite enough," he muttered.

"What?" Surely, I misheard.

"Coffee. I obviously need some. That's why I'm here." Adam

flashed me another perfect smile and said, "And that's my favorite. Shade grown, toxin free. It's better for you."

He wasn't just making conversation. Adam was a bit intense about his health. No drugs. No cigarettes. Little booze. Organic diet. He was also committed to meditation *and* a rigorous workout schedule of boxing, weightlifting, and running. Somehow, Adam managed to be bad-ass and supremely healthy all at once.

"Uh huh. I've heard the speeches a few times already, Adam. Toxins are bad; organic is good." I was grateful that we switched topics. Thinking about being tattooed by him made me think about being naked with him.

And *that* was a terrible idea.

His only true vice was sex. He's bedded far too many of the ink bunnies who loitered at the tattoo shop. It was easy to see why they threw themselves at him. Looking at him for longer than a minute was enough to make me consider taking a turn in his line of all-too-willing partners. I was his friend—and it would stay that way as long as we didn't fall into bed.

I still let my gaze roam where my hands and lips couldn't. I dreamed of him, and I fantasized about what life would be like if I wasn't such a mess and he was willing to do commitments.

As I tried to keep my thoughts from my expression, Adam repeated his regular question of late: "So . . . when are you coming by Sinners to finish the piece?"

I shrugged as I stacked clean mugs on the counter. I glanced around the shop at the two drunk girls who seemed to be having a heated conversation in a low voice, the customers studying or staring at their laptops, and Mila who was staring at Ian, the hot musician singing to the motley crowd. There were no distractions to save me from the conversation.

It wasn't that I didn't *want* to get my tattoo done, but I had my reasons for putting it off. "Not sure," I muttered.

"I'll be at The Tiger tonight if you want to look at your schedule with me," he offered. "We could catch up. Grab a drink."

I nodded, glancing again at one of the drunk girls who looked like she was going to spew at any minute. Mila was glaring at the girls as if willpower alone would prevent vomit.

"I don't know," I told Adam, who was now standing with his hands on the counter and his gaze on me.

The truth was that I wasn't sure I could handle seeing him tonight, especially at the local dive bar. He never picked up his fling of the moment in front of me, but sometimes I thought that only made it harder to remind myself that he was off limits. My eyes traced over the light gleam of sweat on his biceps and the way the torn black t-shirt clung to his chest and abs. Every inch of his body was so lickably gorgeous that it was hard not to sigh. Adam was built to be sighed over.

That didn't mean he wasn't dangerous. I'd seen him throw down in more than a couple fights. Being a tattooist sometimes meant dealing with an unsavory crowd. Being Tommy's cousin often meant dealing with a bad element. Adam handled the worst of them like an off-duty MMA fighter.

I quickly looked down at a burn mark on the counter before my staring was too obvious. I wished my hair wasn't all pulled back in a braid. It was harder to hide my face without my hair to use as a shield. I wasn't going to ruin our friendship—or Adam's relationship with Tommy—by thinking about Adam's perfect mouth or his obscenely muscular body. Okay, I wasn't going to ruin it by letting him *know* I thought about it. I couldn't really *stop* thinking about him, not entirely. I'd tried.

"As soon as I can," I said. "I promise. I want to get my tattoo finished. I just can't right now."

I didn't tell him why. I knew he thought it was about money, and I let him think that. It wasn't like I had much money to spare. I would for this, but that wasn't the real problem. The tattoo I'd started in January—a series of cherry blossoms and branches that spanned my right side and would eventually stretch under my right breast and ease along my hip—was something I'd wanted for years, but now that we'd reached the part where the next bit was on my chest, I couldn't handle being stretched out topless on Adam's table while his beautiful hands held me in place. It was difficult enough when he was working on my side and back. That one session we'd had where he'd started the outline on my chest had sent me running out the door.

Friends. Friends was good. Friends meant I couldn't allow myself the tremors I felt when his eyes and hands were all about me.

A banging noise in the back drew my attention. I didn't even want to ask who was having sex in the bathroom again. I knew we were a bit of a dive, but really? Sex in the coffee shop bathroom. Ewww.

"We can work something out, Sasha," Adam suggested, once more pulling my attention to him.

I made a noise, not agreeing or arguing. I loved the way he said my real name. No one else used it. Everyone had started calling me Sugar since I took up with Tommy a couple years ago. He had introduced me as Sugar Sweet when I met people, and they mostly figured it was what I wanted to be called. So, Sugar became my name. It was even what I called myself. Adam refused to use it. To him, and him alone, I was still Sasha.

He gave me a strange look that I couldn't read. On someone else, I'd have said it was jealousy, but Adam and I weren't like that. We were friends.

"Are you back with Tommy?" he asked.

I shook my head. My New Year's Resolution this year was to get my shit together. Tommy wasn't willing to do the same, so we split up.

"I'm not with anyone," I told Adam. I met his eyes as I added, "I'm not back on the shit either. Five months."

Adam nodded. "Just asking. I know it's hard, and you've been doing great." He paused and gave me a proud look. "You're strong enough to do anything you want, Sash. Tommy is good people, deep down, but you don't need mixed up in the shit he sells."

I caught Mila watching us then. She was always quick to suggest I should work out my issues by overdosing on the lusciousness that was Adam. She didn't understand that I didn't want to throw Adam's friendship away over a few days of sex.

"I'll call you soon. Promise," I told Adam.

He paid for his coffee—black, no sugar or cream, nothing fancy other than the beans themselves—and then dropped a ten-dollar bill onto the counter. Before he turned away, he added, "You don't have to avoid me because you're too stubborn to let me do your art on credit, you know?"

"Sinners Ink doesn't accept credit," I reminded him.

"The *shop* doesn't, but I would for you, Sasha." He looked at me with the same smoldering gaze that made all the ink bunnies drop to their knees if he gave them half a chance.

"I don't need credit."

"The option's on the table if you change your mind. If you aren't coming by for art, we can still grab a drink or whatever."

"I'm sure you've been busy, and I don't want to get in the way of your social life," I said. He was a great friend, and I didn't want to screw it up by hanging around all the time like I was one of the ink groupies or some girl who chases away all his hook-ups.

"You're never in the way," he said. He shook his head, turned, and left.

I watched him go, wishing things were different. He was beautiful, sweet, and covered with the kind of tattoos that made clothing seem like a crime. There was no way anything could happen with Adam. Not now. Not ever. Neither of us was looking for a relationship. He screwed ink bunnies, and I wasn't ready to lose what I had right now with his. I just needed to keep some space while I got my head around the fact that he was off limits. Our last few tattoo sessions had made that detail absurdly hard to remember. The man was gifted with his hands even when he was just doing his job. It was embarrassing how close I'd come to whimpering simply by being tattooed by him.

AN HOUR LATER, I was so ready to leave work. My boss, Jason, had called to say he would be late coming in to pick up the bank drop for the day, so we could just lock the doors, and he'd let himself in after we closed. It was strange for Jason to leave the bank bag full of cash in the store, but he was a prick, so I wasn't going to wait around for him. In fact, with Jason absent, I might didn't have any plans, but I might even close a few minutes early if we were dead. He'd never know. I'd have to see if Mila, the other barista, would go along with my plan.

Unfortunately, the Coffee Cave wasn't as dead as I wanted it to be. Bars had been spilling into the street, so we had a few of the usual drunk girls, loud and shrill. They were enough to make me remember why I worked at a coffee shop instead of a bar.

It was more bearable some nights when we had music to cover the laughs and voices. Tonight, Ian was playing. Right now, it was a cover of "Hallelujah" by Leonard Cohen. He was a decent guitar player, but it was his voice that made people stop and listen. He had just dropped in when we were short a singer, so we didn't have the usual crowd of devotees that swarmed The Coffee Cave when he was here. If I were the sort to go for rock stars, I'd consider taking a run at him.

The two drunk girls who were making far too much of a

scene of themselves suddenly bolted for the back of the coffee shop where the bathroom was.

Mila stopped swiping her bar-rag over the table long enough to yell, "It's occupied."

She looked my way and rolled her eyes, then she went back to what she was doing while I pasted on my fake smile and turned to the new customer. "What can I get for you?"

He made me want to take a step backward. He was dead-eyed and muscled, but not in the tempting way Adam was. In fact, he made me wish Adam was still here. I'd been in enough shady places the past few years to know that there were people who oozed mean. This guy was one of them.

"Double espresso with orgeat."

I paused, startled. No one had *ever* ordered orgeat in the entire time I'd worked here. I shrugged. Orgeat sounded exotic, but it was really just a sweetened almond flavoring so he was asking for espresso with sugary almond syrup. It was a basic drink to prep, but it sounded fancy if people heard you order it. The man wasn't the biggest jerk I'd served today, but I did want to roll my eyes and scoff at his smarmy pretentiousness.

As I prepared his drink, I looked around the cafe. There were a few people, but the last of the stragglers were starting to pack up—and I really didn't want to be left alone with Mr. Almond Espresso. He looked like I felt when I had been strung out.

"That'll be $3.89," I said.

The man took a sip of his coffee, glared at me as if I'd done something wrong that he just didn't know yet, and took another sip. Then he slid his drink farther down the counter and pulled out his wallet. He paused, his gaze darting around the shop in visible paranoia. Either Almond Espresso was hiding from someone or he was high on something more than espresso.

Mila had finally stopped wiping already-clean tables and was now clearing used mugs and plates from the empty tables; she carried a bin of dirty dishes to the counter and nodded toward the bathroom where the two drunk girls had gone. "I swear, if I have to clean up puke tonight, I'm going to spit in their next coffee next time."

I grinned at her, but I didn't say anything. The drunk co-eds banging on the bathroom door were as much a staple as the over-caffeinated students and the weirdos that wandered in from the bars.

Mr. Almond Espresso looked between us like we were more interesting than we were.

Mila glanced over at Ian who sat on a small raised platform at the front of the shop, absently playing his guitar. "Could you play something that will drown out the sounds of spew?" she called.

When Mila went to check on the two drunks, the man at the counter lunged forward, stretching his arm over the counter, and grabbed my wrist.

I yelped, but not loudly.

"Do you think I'm stupid?" he snarled.

"No?" Fear flashed over me at his tone, but I still didn't struggle. I wasn't sure if that would make things worse or not. I silently added "possible mental disorder" to my list of reasons he was acting so oddly.

"I'm not going to get played." He squeezed my arm and jerked me closer. My feet left the floor as he practically dragged me across the counter.

Mugs toppled to the floor with a crash as I tried to yank my arm out of his grip. Instead of getting free though, I came hurtling over the counter as he dragged me to him.

I stumbled to me feet as soon as he released me, but I was backed against the counter.

"Where is he?" the man asked.

"Who?" I croaked.

Almond Espresso punched me. No warning. Just a fist coming

at me. I twisted and my movement meant his knuckles only grazed my cheek. It still hurt like a bitch.

"Need my purse," I yelled, hoping someone would hear and get it for me. Inside it was the gun I carried for emergencies. This was quickly becoming an emergency.

I tried to dart past him, but he grabbed and shook me. I started to fall to the ground. Only his hand on my arm kept me from falling.

"I don't know what you want," I told him.

"Bullshit."

Almond Espresso's jacket was pulled back, and I could see a black semiautomatic gun in a holster.

He shoved me toward the counter. I hit it and fell to the ground. I knew there were people in the room moving and yelling. I couldn't tell what they were saying though. All I could do was stare at the man with the gun who was furious with me for some reason I didn't understand. In all the times I'd done shit that could've gotten me seriously hurt, I'd never felt the terror that filled me now.

Then I heard a voice say, "Stop it!"

When I looked past the man, I saw one of the regulars (black coffee, one sugar). My purse was at her feet, and in her hands was my unmarked, unregistered revolver. She stood, aiming at the man.

"Mind your business," the man snarled, reaching for his gun.

His hand closed around the grip. He drew it out of the holster.

And then there was a shot.

I screamed, expecting to feel pain. I didn't. I wasn't the one who'd been hit. Black Coffee had shot him.

He fell. It wasn't like in the movies where the bullet was in slow motion. In real life, shootings happen in a single heartbeat. One minute the crazy man was standing over me, and then he was on the floor bleeding.

"Shit!" someone said.

"Oh my God!"

"Is he . . . is he *dead*?"

Everything was suddenly happening all at once.

"Whoever is in this room, is in the room." Ian walked over to the door, threw the lock, and announced, "And we're not leaving until we sort this shit out."

I walked over and carefully took my gun from Black Coffee. I shoved the revolver inside my purse.

"It's okay," I whispered to her. Then, louder, I said, "Everything's going to be okay."

"We should call the police," a guy said.

"Absolutely not."

I didn't want to get caught with an unregistered gun that was undoubtedly tied to something illegal before it was in my possession and oh yeah, had just been used to kill a guy.

No one spoke. It was like we were in a collective state of shock.

"Okay." I squatted down and patted the dead guy down for car keys.

Once I located the keys, I concentrated on ignoring the sick feeling I had from rifling through the pockets of a dead man.

"Sugar?" Mila said.

"No one else comes inside."

Then I went out to the lot, pushed the remote until a car's lights flicked on, and went over to the nondescript blue sedan. I popped the trunk so we could see if there was room for the body and . . . stopped. Inside the trunk were a bunch of black duffle bags. I had a bad feeling about what that meant, and it only got worse when I unzipped one, and then another, and then one more. After a moment, I breathed, "Fuck!"

"Now what?" Black Coffee asked in a low voice from behind me.

I scowled at her. "Why aren't you inside?"

"Needed air," she said with a shrug.

I looked around. The street was clear, and there were no lights anywhere. We were lucky.

"Help me?"

We both grabbed a couple bags and went back inside.

"Close the blinds," I ordered when we were back inside. I felt stupid for not saying that before, but no one came in while we were standing around the corpse so we were still okay.

Black Coffee dropped the bags on the floor, well away from the blood. "This was in the trunk."

Ian squatted down and opened two of the bags.

No one said anything at first but then I said, "Look, with this much money, someone will come looking for him." I nodded toward the dead man. "We split this evenly and no one ever comes back here again. No cops. No talking. Take the money and get gone."

"I don't want it," someone said. "I don't want *any* of his money."

"Everyone takes it. It makes us all equally guilty," Mila added. "We all take our share of the money. We never come back here. Cut ties and stay away from this place. And we don't talk to anyone else who was here. Deal?"

Black Coffee unzipped the rest of the bags. Everyone was looking at the money. There was a *lot* of it.

"Deal," I echoed.

Everyone else repeated it, some more quickly and some in whispers that sounded very reluctant. It didn't matter, though: They all agreed.

As Black Coffee started pulling out stacks of hundred dollar bills, she stopped and pulled out something else. There were two kilos of cocaine in the fifth bag.

"We need to do something with this," she said, holding up a brick of coke.

"I'll take it," I said in my calmest voice.

"Why *you*?" Ian asked.

"We can split it, too, if you want," I suggested, but after a moment of silence, it was obvious that no one else actually wanted it.

We counted the money, and then we divided it equally—$210,000 each—and then the drunk girls drove off in the dead guy's car with him in the trunk. They got an extra $20,000 for getting rid of the body and the car. Soon, the body, the blood, the car, the drugs, and the money were all gone.

And we were all a part of it.

ADAM

Adam walked into one of the local dive bars he'd frequent regularly the past couple of years. Even though it was named for a Prohibition speakeasy, the Blind Tiger was far from classy or unique. It felt like the sort of bar he'd been inside in more towns than he could remember—dark, worn, and comfortable. It was a lot more comfortable when he had Sasha with him, but she was still at work.

He had what his Aunt Grace and mother called "itchy feet." He liked to roam. Being a tattoo artist made that possible. He packed his essentials, his work gear, and went where the road led him. A few years ago, the road took him west, and his aunt's worrying took him into Rio Verde to check on his cousin.

The interior of the bar was dark enough that it was easy to blend into the shadows of a corner if you had a mind to do so, and the crowd was a mix of denim, leather, and flashes of color on the short-skirted girls hanging on the arms of the blue-collar guys that clustered here. Places like this felt like home. No matter what state they were in, they were the same. The beer was cold, and the whiskey was a generous pour. When Adam hopped his way from state to state, he always found a few dives that he liked. The Blind Tiger was one of the ones he liked best in Rio Verde. Too many of the rest were co-ed hang-outs or sports bars. The Tiger was more his speed.

Sometimes he thought about going where there were Southern Wolves, but the desert suited him better than the South did these days. He still wore his Southern Wolves patches prominently, but his also read: Nomad. He missed being part of the camaraderie of a motorcycle club, but his life was better these days. No trouble. Just tattoos, open roads, and the occasional one-night stand.

Adam made his way to a table where he could sit with his back to the wall and surveyed the crowd surreptitiously. It was a habit he couldn't shake. He might steer clear of trouble, but that didn't mean that he forgot that there was always at least one dumbass in most every bar just waiting for a chance to prove something.

"Johnnie Walker Black," he said as the barmaid approached.

She smiled in a friendly way, and Adam wondered if he'd slept with her at some point and forgotten. He had spells where he went through far more women than maybe he ought to, but there was only so much he could drink without feeling like he was too near out of control. He didn't touch drugs anymore, hadn't in years. That left one good, or maybe bad, choice for getting outside his mind. Sex. No strings, no lies, no promises. He made sure the women he fucked got as good as they gave, or better. If any of them were more into giving than getting, he made sure to get their name and number so he could even the score later. If they gave him pleasure, he owed them the same. It was simple math.

Unfortunately, it had become a little awkward after a few years in the same town. He didn't usually stay this long, and Rio Verde wasn't an enormous place. Luckily, there were enough co-eds who were in and out because of ASU Rio Verde that he had renewable resources every year.

"You haven't been around much lately," the barmaid said as she returned with his drink.

"Work's been good," he said as a sort of excuse.

She opened her mouth to say something else, but was interrupted by his cousin walking up behind her and patting her ass. She spun to face him. "What the hell?"

"Bud and a glass of Jack and Coke," Tommy said. He held out a twenty. "No change."

Whatever other complaints she was going to raise vanished as she took the crinkled bill out of his hand.

Tommy pulled out a chair, spun it around, and straddled it. It was a leftover habit from their childhood that he never quite gave up as an adult. "Is she yours?"

Adam sighed. "I may have gotten to know her at some point. I'm not sure."

"Not memorable then?" Tommy looked over toward the bar. "Shame. I've been feeling out of sorts without Sugar around."

At the mention of the girl Adam coveted, he tensed. He didn't comment, though. He was sure Tommy suspected Adam's interest in Sasha, but he didn't ever point it out. They were family, and that meant they had a tacit agreement to ignore uncomfortable things when necessary.

If they weren't family, Adam knew he and Tommy wouldn't be sitting at a table together. *Ever.* They were opposites in both the obvious and less obvious ways. Adam was health conscious, believed in hard work, and vowed never to snort or shoot poison again. Tommy was a walking, schmoozing, bad habit. He liked a buffet of toxins—pot, cigarettes, coke, molly, speed. If he could turn a profit on it or have a good weekend using it, Tommy was game. They looked different enough that no one would mistake them for the family they were either. Tommy was wiry, and Adam had the sort of mass that came from weight training. The both had the family eyes, bright blue that people remarked on regularly. If not for that, there was no resemblance in their appearances.

"Was Sugar working tonight?" Tommy asked in the tone that said he already knew the answer *and* knew that Adam had been by the Coffee Cave.

"She was."

Tommy nodded. "She seem okay?"

And there was the one thing they *did* have in common: They both cared about Sasha. Tommy might be a louse, but he was a louse in love—or as close to it as he could get. Adam didn't blame him. Just the sight of Sasha with her tumble of dark curls and painfully thin frame got him so bothered that he was sitting here instead of home where he should be.

"She seemed fine," Adam said, sipping his whisky to keep from starting in on the old arguments. He swore sometimes that the more he suggested Tommy let Sasha alone, the more he clung to her.

"It's been weeks since she came around." Tommy propped his feet on the table and rocked his chair back on two legs. "Did she mention anyone new?"

Adam wanted to say that there *was* someone new—him—but that wasn't true, despite his hopes. "I'm not your spy."

"You *are* my cousin," Tommy said.

"And Sasha's friend."

"So did *Sugar* mention seeing anyone?" Tommy watched him, as if he was actually able to intimidate Adam. It might've worked on a lot of people, but Adam outweighed Tommy and had been fighting for a lot longer. He wasn't intimidated by much of anyone at this point in his life.

"No."

Tommy nodded. "Then she'll be back. She's like a feral cat. She needs some leash, and then she'll come home."

Adam drained his whisky to keep himself from saying something ugly to his cousin.

"She's acting like we're done, but she's kept her sheets empty." Tommy grinned. "It's like a vacation. A break. She'll come home."

The words Adam wanted to say weren't his right. He'd thought she was finally going to admit that she was interested in him, too, the last time she'd come in to get tattooed. Instead, she'd walked out afterward, and she'd dodged his attempts to even sit down for a conversation. No more after-work-drinks. No lunches. No stopping by the shop with a coffee for him. She had done the exact opposite of what he wanted. He was left feeling like a stalker stopping in the Coffee Cave to see if she was around. It was a business and he liked coffee, so it wasn't a real surprise that he went there, but she had to have noticed that he came around more lately.

He'd hoped that she'd show up tonight even though she hadn't agreed when he'd asked, but now that he was sitting here with Tommy, Adam was almost hoping she wouldn't come. Not entirely. He'd prefer Tommy heading out, and *then* Sasha showing up.

She made him think about things like a real home, roots and mortgages, all of those things that he was sure he'd never want. Even if he couldn't have them with her, he sure as hell wasn't going to watch her destroy herself with Tommy. Adam debated how to handle the jealousy and protectiveness that roiled inside him.

"You still here?" Tommy asked.

"Yeah. Long week. A bunch of things on my mind," Adam said blandly. He sipped his drink and looked around the bar. "What's up with you?"

Tommy shrugged. "Just chillin' and handling business."

"You know, Aunt Gracie worries. You should call her," Adam suggested. "Or at least come up with better lies when you talk to her. She *knows* you're not really taking any classes at the university. Why'd you tell her that?"

"Slept with a few girls in business classes. They left textbooks on my table." Tommy shook his head and then flashed a huge smile at Adam. "I wasn't lying either. I said I was studying some things about business majors . . . I just didn't say those things were girls."

"Well, be a little more realistic with her. You lie to her; she calls my mother, and *she* calls me."

The cocktail waitress came back around with another round of drinks. Tommy patted her ass again and over-tipped her. He didn't need to tell Adam that he'd turned a deal of some sort. He always waved his money around when he did.

Adam silently accepted the drink and pretended not to notice the way the waitress was cozying up to Tommy now. Maybe he'd leave early with her, and that way if Sasha showed up there wouldn't be a scene. Coke, booze, and a willing girl were Tommy's standard good night, but if he could mix in a jealous Sasha, he'd call it a great night.

"Lila," Adam said, having heard her name called by another patron, "have you met my cousin, Tommy?"

She smiled at Tommy. "Not officially."

"Tommy, this is Lila. Lila, Tommy."

The two exchanged appraising looks, and Adam figured that he could expect Tommy to leave whenever Lila was done for the night. He hoped that they'd leave before the bar closed. Hopefully, they'd go before Sasha showed up . . . if she was going to show at all.

While Tommy and Lila bantered, Adam tuned them out and wondered what else he could do to make Sasha understand that he was interested in her. He'd never had to work for a girl's attention, and he felt almost embarrassingly unsure of how to do so. He didn't want to come on too strong.

Adam's attention returned to the bar when he heard Lila say, "I can probably take off since we're so dead."

Tommy dropped two more twenty-dollar bills on the table. "Get us another round first."

Adam tried not to let his disdain show. Tommy wasn't a bad guy. He just lacked common sense.

When Lila returned a few minutes later, Tommy slammed his drink, looped an arm around her, and they left. They weren't even out the door when Adam's shoulders relaxed. Being around Tommy always made him tense, but even when Adam was ready to smack his cousin up alongside the head, he wasn't going to let anyone else do it. Family stuck together.

Now that he was alone at his table with one more drink than he needed, he settled in to wait and hope.

He knew that The Coffee Cave closed soon, but he figured it was crossing a line from friend to stalker if he went back there now. He glanced at the door furtively and scanned the bar again. If she didn't come soon, he was going to have to admit defeat.

For tonight.

SUGAR

I wasn't sure what to do with the cocaine and my share of the cash. Time in prison orange wasn't high on my list of life goals.

It wasn't any wonder then that I was shaking when I left The Coffee Cave. I was shaking a hell of a lot worse when I got to my place. I stashed the money and the coke, took a quick shower, and grabbed a few necessities. I left my hair hanging loose around my face and shoulders to hide the already forming bruise from when I was punched. In less than a half hour I was ready to walk back out my door. I knew Tommy was likely asleep, but I still hurried like he was awake and waiting.

This was so far off the path I wanted to be on. I'd moved to Rio Verde because that's where my money ran out, and I hadn't really had a destination in mind beyond "not in Ohio." My parents weren't awful. They just drank and didn't have much use for a kid. I could've stayed with them when I turned eighteen, but paying rent to live in nowhere, Ohio seemed stupid. There was nothing for me in Ohio. So I left. I stayed in touch some at first, but five years later, I was in my own dead-end life in Arizona and hearing my mother mock me sent me into spirals of bad moods, so I stopped calling.

I *wanted* a better future, a little house, a good man, and maybe a bit of travel. I could even deal with a meaningless job if I had the house and the man. That's all I really wanted out of life. It sounded so simple, but it seemed as elusive as a mansion in the sky.

Or maybe I just didn't know how to get it. What I knew was mostly things that were bad for me—like Tommy. He was like a big plate of dessert. I knew he was bad for me, but sometimes in the middle of the night, I still ended up wanting a piece more than anything. We'd been on again off again for a little over two years now. We were bad together in everything but sex. He kept saying he loved me, and maybe he did, but I didn't want to spend the rest of my life in Rio Verde or end up in jail because I got caught up in one of his business ventures.

Not that my own actions tonight weren't beyond illegal. A man was killed. A group of people were complicit in hiding the death of a drug dealer and theft of what was undoubtedly drug money. Oh, and I had what I thought was about fifty thousand dollars of cocaine in my possession. If I got caught by the cops, I would go to jail for a list of felonies, and if I were found by the owner of the drugs, I'd be dead by morning. In a few short hours, everything had changed. Now, it wasn't Tommy that was the danger to my freedom and life. *I* was the problem.

Which gave me a good excuse to ignore every reason I had to stay clear of Tommy. He was no good for me for so many reasons, but right now, I needed his help desperately. I didn't love him, but I cared about him a lot, and I trusted him. There was no one else I could go to with that kind of drugs. I'd stashed the money at my apartment before I brought the drugs to him, to the apartment that used to be mine too.

Right now I needed to see Tommy. It wasn't just his help I

wanted; I needed *him*. He was the closest thing to a friend I had—other than Adam. I couldn't tell Adam what I did. I'd be mortified if he knew how much of a disaster I'd gotten twisted up in tonight.

I needed a friend tonight, so I could forget that terrible few minutes earlier. Having a pile of cash wouldn't do anything to make me forget that just a couple of hours ago, I thought I might die. There was a man, a gun, and a fist. Cash, even over a hundred grand, didn't make that okay with me. I wasn't close to my parents, and the only friends I had were Tommy and Adam. I needed to be around someone I trusted, even if it was just for a few hours. Then, after I got rid of the coke, I needed to get out of town.

I pounded on the door, not caring if anyone heard and pretty damn sure that the only way he'd bother answering was if he thought there was something in it for him. "Open up! It's Sugar!"

A few minutes of yelling and pounding on the door passed before I heard the locks slide and click. Then the door was open, and he stood there in front of me. He'd obviously been sleeping. No shirt. No shoes. Pants slung low on his hips. Nothing but dark tattoos, tight muscles, and bare skin—it didn't help that he had the same deep blue eyes that lit up Adam's face. Like I said, he was dessert I shouldn't have. It took my few remaining threads of self-control not to launch myself at him.

"What the fuck, Sugar? It's the middle of the night and—"

"Are you alone?"

He ran his hand up his cheek and rubbed his face. "Yeah."

I pushed past him into his tiny apartment. A few empty long-neck bottles rattled as they fell and rolled across the coffee table I must have bumped. Behind me, I could hear the door close, and the locks engage.

"So you get an itch in the middle of the night and figure it don't matter what I've got going on?" He flopped down on the battered sofa and grabbed a pack of Marlboro reds off the table.

I didn't answer. Not yet. I'd let him have his say before I told him how severely I'd fucked my life tonight.

The familiar click of his lighter was followed by the glow of a cigarette he didn't bother to offer me. "What if I had someone here? You say you're done with me, but you still storm in here at all hours. Maybe you ought to take your key back if this is the way it's going to be. There's a hell of a lot nicer ways you could've woken me than banging on my door."

"I need to move something," I blurted. "Big."

He stared at me silently then. The only noise was the soft crackle of burning tobacco and the quiet whoosh of him exhaling smoke.

"Some guy left his bag in the shop and . . . I figured you could help me. I'll give you as much a cut of the sale as you need."

"How much are we talking about?"

"Two bricks."

"Damn. How pure?"

I shrugged.

"That's right. You're 'clean' again." He shook his head at that, but his vice was bitter. My decision to stay away from him was all tangled up in my decision to stay away from coke. Tommy wasn't very happy about it. Every time I'd run into him the past few months, he'd mentioned it. It didn't stop him from offering me a taste of the coke he always had on hand. So far I'd always said no to the coke every time.

"I can't sell what I can't taste, Sugar Girl," Tommy said.

I pulled out the bricks that I'd shoved into my purse before I'd left my apartment and dropped it on the table in front of him. Neither of us mentioned the way my hands shook when I did so.

"Doesn't look like you even opened it."

I shrugged.

He cut one and licked a bit of the cocaine from his knife, looked up at me, and then got to business. I watched him as he poured it out, lined it up, and inhaled. Somewhere in those few moments, I'd crossed my arms. I didn't even realize I'd done it until I felt the edges of my fingernails dig into the skin of my arms.

Tommy leaned back on his sofa and watched me. "Someone's definitely going to be missing this."

"Will you sell it for me?"

He nodded.

I forced myself to stare only at him, not on the remaining three lines he'd drawn on the table. I knew the smaller one off to the side was for me if I wanted it. I could say no, and he'd be fine with it. I also knew that tonight of all nights I wanted that bliss more than ever. Still, I reminded us both, "I quit."

He smiled at me. "You quit a lot of things, but you don't stay quit."

"I quit," I repeated.

"You want it or not?" He nodded toward the table. "Say the word."

I swallowed. Of course, I *wanted* it. Tommy was one of those weird people who could do a bump here or there, but stop. He had a lot more control than I did.

I swallowed again and shook my head. I couldn't speak the lie aloud tonight.

"I'll help you get rid of it," he promised. Then he was standing beside me, arm around my waist. He pushed my hair aside and, almost at the same moment, had his lips on that spot on the side of my throat that he knew I liked too much.

"Tomorrow," I said. "You can't keep this very long, Tommy. It's got to get gone as fast as you can."

"I want thirty percent for selling it."

"Done." I glanced back at the line on the table. It was ridiculous that a tiny white line was that hard to look away from, but it was. I pulled away from Tommy. He needed to finish that before I gave in.

He bent down and inhaled one of the remaining lines. "It's barely cut. Purest I've tasted in a while."

"I quit."

"Your choice, Sugar Girl, but"—he plucked at my shirt, trying to pull it off—"I'm not going to be sleeping."

"I didn't come here for that." I paused, met his eyes, and admitted, "I just needed a friend, someone I can trust."

"You can trust me, Sugar."

"I just need a friend," I stressed. "We don't work."

He pointed looked at the drugs. "Because you have other plans for your life." He looked at me. "I see that."

"I'm leaving town as soon as you sell it." I must have sounded sincere because he looked alarmed.

"Move back in with me," Tommy demanded.

There was no good answer to that. I couldn't say yes. I leaned forward and kissed him.

After a few minutes, he jerked away from my kiss and repeated, "Move back in with me."

"No."

"I'll keep you safe," he swore, and I knew he believed it.

Staying here, being in this town, being with him. . . none if that was going to lead to safety.

I whispered. "Can you be my friend tonight?"

He gave in and grabbed the television remote. "Fine."

My hair fell over my shoulder and brushed against his face as I kissed his cheek.

"Love you," he muttered as he pulled me in for a hug.

When I didn't say anything, he wrapped an arm around me and held me to his side. "You could sleep here."

"I got to go home and pack," I whispered. "You need to get rid of it for me. Quick. No more than a day, Tommy. Then I'm gone. Whoever it belonged to won't ever find me."

I tried not to think about what happened a few hours ago. A man died, killed with my gun, and I couldn't go back to that job except to quit. I didn't have any savings, and I needed to leave Rio Verde. I wasn't sure what I'd use to run if not for the dead man's money, but I walked out of the night's mistakes with thousands of dollars and a good quantity of coke. I had enough money to be long gone when someone came around asking questions. I just needed Tommy to get rid of the coke first. He'd turn it into money, and I'd run.

SUGAR

I had no more than left Tommy's apartment and walked into the lot when I saw Adam.

"You visiting Tommy?"

I shook my head. "Not like that."

Adam stared at me like he wanted to believe me, but he wasn't sure he could. He glanced at the sky. Morning wasn't far off, and I was leaving Tommy's place.

"It's not him I want," I blurted out.

"Oh?"

I laughed. After months of pretending I wasn't interested, I was admitting it. Why not, though? I was leaving in less than two days. Why not tell Adam the truth? If not now, it wouldn't ever happen. I'd be long gone.

"You can't tell me you didn't notice," I said louder than I meant to. "I can barely stop looking at you."

He made a "carry on" gesture.

"I want you, Adam. I wanted you before I left Tommy. I wanted you after I left." I put my hand flat on his chest. "I want you right now. Right here." I motioned to the building. "You could fuck me against the wall."

"Are you high?"

I laughed until tears spilled out of my eyes. "Sober. No booze. No coke. Just . . . shaken."

Adam looked up at Tommy's building. "Did he hurt you?"

"No." I swallowed. "There were drugs. I was tempted. God, I was tempted. I said no to them, to him, but maybe . . . maybe I need something else. *Someone* else. Maybe I thought if I told you that it's you I picture when I'm alone in my bed and touch myself . . ."

He took a step closer and in a low growl of a voice asked, "Do you now?"

"I do. I think about you. Inside me. Touching me." I stare at him, holding his gaze, and added, "Licking me."

For a moment, Adam stared back at me. Then he said, "Let's go."

Mutely, I obeyed. I wasn't sure if he was walking me home or what, but I wasn't going to ask. Did he reject me? Did he think I wanted to use him? He wasn't entirely wrong. I wanted him because I cared and because he really was everything I fantasized about—and not just alone in my bed. When I dreamed of a future, he was the one I wanted at my side. For meals. For quiet nights watching television. For every day. I couldn't have that, not now.

Maybe, though, I could have one night.

After two blocks, we turned and I realized that he was leading us to his place.

Inside the door, he flipped on a light and stood staring at me. "If you just want a safe place to be—"

"I want you."

"And you swear to me that you are completely sober? You're . . . my friend, Sasha. I don't want to take advantage of you." He looked like he was struggling to look at me. "If you're not sure or . . ."

I pulled off my shirt.

"Sash . . . ?" He fisted his hands at his sides.

I unhooked my bra and let it drop.

"Are you sure?"

I stepped closer to him and unbuttoned my jeans. "Do I have to touch myself again tonight?"

Adam made an animal noise and pulled me in for a kiss. Mouth slashing over mine, hands gripping my hips. It was even better than my fantasies.

When he pulled back, all I could say was, "More."

He stared, motionless, and I started to walk away. Before I made it three steps, Adam was behind me.

I froze,

He lifted my hair, draping it over one shoulder as he kissed down my spine and worked my jeans and underwear off my hips. I couldn't move if I wanted to, not that I wanted to. I wanted to be consumed. I wanted to feel everything.

Just one night.

I shoved thoughts of earlier tonight, of dead men and drugs, away. I was with *Adam* tonight. Adam would never be mine for real, but I was taking tonight.

In moments I was bent over a chair with Adam behind me. I was dripping already. "Yes," I said, loudly enough that there was no doubt. "Fuck me, Adam."

He said nothing, but in another heartbeat, he slid inside me with a sigh.

"Fucking *wanted* you for so long, Sasha," he said between thrusts.

"Same," I managed.

He paused. My body clenched around his cock, and he demanded, "Really?"

I closed my eyes, letting myself surrender to some truth at least, and said, "No one else has touched me . . . not even Tom--"

He pulled out, making me whimper at the loss. "Honestly?"

I nodded, dropped to my knees and stared up at him. If he wouldn't fuck me, I could at least have a taste. I leaned forward and opened my mouth.

"Sasha!"

I made a noise, a purr, around him as I eased forward and took the length of him as far as I could manage.

Instead of letting me have me way, a few moments later, Adam pushed me onto my back on his living room floor. Then, he was back inside me, and I had to hold onto the underside of the sofa to keep from being turned into a mess of carpet-burn.

He paused, grabbed my legs, and forced them as high as he could. My legs were straight in the air, my ankles were by his head, and he was deep inside me. It felt amazing, but it was a devil's brand of heaven. Every bit of pleasure was tainted with guilt—I was using Adam, and I'd be gone before the week was out.

One night. Just one night.

By the time my arms ached from holding myself steady against the sofa and my leg muscles were shaking from being up in the air so long, he'd made me come twice.

No matter how awful I'd feel tomorrow, my body still felt sated.

I was shaking all over, and he was still rock hard and in control. He stopped moving again. He pulled out, ignoring my cry of loss, and asked, "Who do you want?"

"You," I whispered. "Only you."

All he said in reply was one word: "Bed."

I didn't move.

I didn't argue.

He lifted me and carried me the short distance to his bed.

"Yes, Adam." I unwrapped my arms from around his neck. "I want this. All of you. All night."

That, at least, was true. *All night.* That I could do. I wasn't promising tomorrow.

Adam gently lowered me to the bed and crawled on the mattress toward me.

"All night," he repeated with a smile.

Then he grabbed my legs, lifted me, and drove into me again.

But, then, just as suddenly as he'd entered me, he stopped. His movements became slow, like we were making love instead of fucking. Slow wasn't what I could handle, not tonight. I needed to let this be meaningless.

"More." I urged him closer, faster, harder.

He slid slowly in and out of my body. "I want to savor this."

"Next time," I lied.

There would be no next time. There was no future. Later, Adam would realize I lied, used him, but tonight he smiled in a kind of wonder.

"Next time," he repeated.

I didn't deserve Adam, but in that moment, I was going to tell him the truth. "I only want you, but tonight . . ."

He sped up, moving hard, deep, and fast.

I wrapped my arms around him, crying out.

Within minutes, I was sobbing and shaking. Again and again, I orgasmed, until finally, he did, too.

Afterward, he held me against his chest.

"Thank you," I whispered.

Adam looked at me then asked, "Do you want to tell me what *else* happened tonight? I'm not a fool, Sasha."

"I can't." I shook my head. "Not right now."

I was trembling so much that my words sounded shaky. "I swear I didn't lie, though. I am sober, and I . . ." My voice broke. "I have wanted you forever."

He held me closer.

Adam was patient, and good, and kind, but I wasn't sure I

could handle that. I wanted to forget the murder, forget the dangers. I'd only have this one night with Adam, and I wasn't going to waste it in tears and talk.

When my shaking stopped, I let my hand roam, touching and stroking him until he was hard again.

"Mmm, stamina," I murmured.

He laughed, low and dark and delicious. "You said *all* night."

"I did." I rolled on top of him. "As long as you're up to it . . ."

LATER AS DAWN ARRIVED, I walked gingerly to the bathroom, I winced. I had more orgasms the past three hours than I'd had throughout the whole last month, and my body ached from it. It was a good kind of tender, but that didn't change the fact that I was walking as if I'd been horseback riding all day.

I smiled at the thought. Despite living in Arizona, I hadn't been on a horse for years. Maybe Adam and I—

I caught myself. There was no "Adam and I." This ended tonight. Now, in fact. I killed the light and went back into the bedroom. Adam was sprawled out on the bed, still naked.

He watched me as I fumbled for a cigarette.

"Talk to me Sasha." He patted the mattress beside him. "Come to bed for a while."

I walked farther into the room, but not all the way to the bed. "I can't do this."

He sat up, pulled the still unlit-cigarette out of my hand, and crushed it. "Do *what?*"

"This." I gestured at him and then at myself. "You."

Adam stared at me.

I stepped closer, meaning to kiss him goodbye. "This was a mistake and—"

He grabbed me and yanked me onto him. Instead of sliding

into me like I expected, he put a hand on either hip and ordered, "Up."

He guided me up his body with firm hands until I was kneeling over his chest.

"Hands on the head board."

"You don't need to—"

"Hands on the head board."

Once I obeyed, he slid down farther so I was straddling his face. I wanted to argue. I wanted to run, but his tongue was amazing.

My hands tightened on the headboard while he licked and sucked. My hair fell over my face as I bowed my head.

He was gentle with me.

I didn't want soft touches, even though I was sore. I didn't want proof that he was generous and loving. My heart hurt even as my body sang.

I took one hand off the headboard, holding myself steady with the other and reaching back to stroke him with my right hand. He groaned and arched into my hand instead of stopping me.

He licked slower.

I tried to push against him, but he held me up so I couldn't get the pressure I wanted.

I removed my hand, and in an instant, he had slid me down his body and slipped inside me. Even now that I was on top, he was the one in control.

I looked down at him and met his eyes.

"I want *you*, but I'm not staying," I insisted.

He pressed his lips together.

I couldn't say the words he wanted. I *wouldn't* love him. I couldn't stay around him when someone was probably already looking for me because of the drugs. I couldn't stay around him. If I did, I'd be endangering him. It was that simple.

"I *need* you," I whispered. "Right now. Please, Adam?"

He stared up at me like he could find words written in my face.

I canted toward him. "I want you."

Adam gave in. Not only did he thrust up, but he let go of my hips, letting me fuck him instead of controlling me, letting me make him lose control for a change.

I slid my hands up his stomach and chest, settling them on his shoulders, and leaned down to kiss him. My hair fell over my shoulder and brushed against his face.

He reached between us and fingered my clit, making me gasp into his mouth, and I started moving again, *slowly*, oh so very slowly for the first time. I didn't speed up even as his fingers danced faster and faster. I kept kissing him because I needed to keep him from saying more words I didn't want to hear. I only stopped kissing him as my orgasm crashed over me.

A moment later, he followed me over, and once spent, he pulled me tighter to him.

"Stay," he muttered against my throat.

When I didn't say anything, he wrapped an arm around me and held me to his chest. "You *can* stay."

I didn't say anything. It was already daylight. I needed to pack, quit my job, and then I needed to go get the cash from Tommy. I wasn't going to Adam any of that, though.

A few moment passed, and then he said, "And Sash?"

"Yeah?"

He brushed my hair back and gently trailed his finger along my jaw. "Don't think I didn't see these bruises on your face and your arms. I want answers."

My breath hitched at his words.

"You don't have to tell me what really happened tonight, but .. . Tomorrow."

"Tomorrow," I echoed.

"We can work it out. Whatever it is," he said in the same voice he'd used when I'd panicked in the past. "Everything will be okay."

"Right," I said, but I was fairly sure we both knew I was lying.

I tried not to think about what happened a few hours ago. A man died, killed with my gun, and I couldn't go back to that job except to quit. I didn't have any savings, and I needed to leave Rio Verde. I wasn't sure what I'd use to run if not for the dead man's money, but I walked out of the night's mistakes with thousands of dollars and a good quantity of coke. I had enough money to be long gone when someone came around asking questions.

I just needed Tommy to get rid of the coke first. He'd turn it into money, and I'd run. On my own. Without spending the night with Adam ever again. I'd leave both the man whose arms I was in and the man who was selling my stolen drugs. No one was going to get hurt because of me.

SUGAR

I decided to slip out of Adam's place only a couple hours later. I kept thinking about the cash that was currently hidden in the box of Rice Krispies at my apartment. It wasn't the most original hiding place, but there wasn't anyone who'd be in my place without me. I wasn't the kind of person who passed out keys to my place even to my close friends. No pets. No plants. If I wasn't there, there was no reason for anyone to go into my apartment. If I was there, any guests could knock on the door.

I called Tommy. "Well?"

"I'll bring the money or the coke back tonight," he promised.

"Be careful, okay?" I flashed back to the man who'd died last night. People don't carry that kind of cash and coke without their absence getting noticed. I was pretty sure we were fast enough to be safe, but soon I wouldn't be. Would they go looking for Tommy when they couldn't find me? If they figured out that I'd taken the coke, it wasn't hard to draw a line from me to Tommy. He was a small-time dealer, and we'd been more or less together for a couple years.

If I left him, they'd find him. I owed him a way out of this life too. Maybe we could save one another, start over and be better people. People can change, right?

Quietly, I asked, "What if we had enough money to go away from here, to start over, to not have to have any drugs around *at all*, would you do it?"

He laughed. "The money from two keys isn't going to be enough forever. Maybe I could re-invest it and--"

"What if there was more?" I squirmed as I said it.

He grew quiet for a minute before asking, "How much more, Sugar?"

"Three times more, maybe," I said. "Cash. If I could get another hundred thousand dollars . . . could you promise no more drugs?"

"Pack your bags, Sugar Sweet," he said cheerily. "I'll go make this last sale, and we'll get out of here tomorrow."

"Ok."

"I knew you'd come back to me," he said.

"Tomorrow we go," I said, and then I hung up.

I didn't tell him I didn't mean that we'd be *together*. I just needed to get him to safety. Now that I was calmer, I realized that I had to save him. Everyone knew Adam wasn't into drugs, and once Tommy was gone, Adam would leave town. I just needed to get Tommy to a new town, let him get a fresh start, and then I'd move on.

I went to my place, closed the door, locked it, and leaned against it. I didn't love Tommy. I'm not sure I ever had, but I owed it to him to save him if I could

After a few moments, I pushed off the door. I was too on edge to try to sleep again, even though I knew I should.

I called Mila.

"Are you okay?" she asked as soon as she answered.

"Sure," I lied.

"What are you going to do?"

I shrugged, even though I was alone in the apartment. "Go in to quit when they open. Jason should be there."

"Do you think the prick is actually in? I need to quit too."

There was no way this wasn't going to look suspicious, but I wasn't going to be able to work at The Coffee Cave even if I could get past the fear of the owner of the coke and money showing up. Images of being jerked over the bar flashed through my mind again. I'd really thought he was going to kill me when I saw the gun under his jacket.

"Text me when you go in so I know if he's there," Mila said. "Maybe I should just call."

"I'm going in . . . I need to. I need to see it without the . . . without that on the floor. Maybe it'll get it out of my head." I paced to my bedroom and started pulling out things that I didn't want to leave behind. I wasn't going to be able to take everything. Clothes. Shoes. Pictures. Those were going into suitcases, but I couldn't take everything.

I flopped down on my bed while Mila talked.

I didn't know how to sort everything out to leave town. Should I leave my stuff behind and replace it? Should I come back for it later? I hopped back to my feet and dragged out my two suitcases. Then I started tossing clothes I *needed* to take with me onto the bed.

We talked for a few minutes while I sorted out the things I wanted to take and the ones I could stand leaving behind. Then I told her, "I'm going away tomorrow or the next day. If anything happens that I need to know, call me, okay?"

She was the one who said it was a bad idea to talk to anyone who was there, but talking to Mila was different. We weren't talking because of the guy in the shop or the money. We talked *before* all of that. We were friends.

We hung up, and I spent the next two hours packing what I could. I wasn't going to look backward after today. I was going to turn my life around. I was going to save Tommy too. We'd both be better after we got away from Rio Verde.

SUGAR

I left my hair loose to hide the bruise on my face. I'd put make-up on too, but even the best concealer and foundation I'd found didn't hide bruises perfectly—and I'd tried quite a few of them while dating Tommy. He'd never once raised a hand to me in anger, but he'd left more marks on me during sex than I would ever want to count. Concealer, foundation, long hair, and long sleeves: that was the uniform of a girl who had things to hide. I changed into a long-sleeved shirt with a ruffle around the wrists.

It was unsettling walking into The Coffee Cave in the harsh desert daylight after what had happened here less than twelve hours ago. The shop always looked a little more worn out during the day, but today was worse. I couldn't help glancing at the very clean floor where the drug dealer had died.

We robbed a dead man.

We hid the murder.

I shivered. Memories, guilt, and withdrawal were a shitty combination.

"It's not payday," Jason said when I walked toward the back room where he sat. He looked almost comical as he sat at a brightly painted, wooden desk. Like everything in the shop—including the employees—it had seen better days.

"I know."

I walked farther into the room. Jason watched me with an expressionless face. He was a weasel of a man, the sort of guy who wore his penny-pinching like a badge of honor. I wouldn't be surprised if he instituted pat downs at the door or a video camera to catch us if we gave away free coffee. . . . Suddenly, my heart stuttered. My hands grew damp. *Did* he have a camera? I wouldn't put it past him. I stared at him in silence, trying to figure out if there was any way to ask. I was pretty sure there wasn't.

"What do you need, Sugar? I'm short staffed tonight, and—"

"I quit," I blurted out.

His lips pressed tightly together as he stared at me. He reached up and pinched the bridge of his nose. Then he said, "Okay, so I need to find *two* baristas in two weeks, and right before summer when all the coeds leave. Great."

"I quit *now*," I amended.

"No."

I looked at him. He was an average man. He wasn't ugly. He could even be funny sometimes. I felt a twinge of guilt at leaving him in the lurch.

Then I thought about the cash, the drugs, and the dead man; the likelihood of someone coming looking for all three was high. If Jason had a camera and saw what was on there, he'd either turn it over to the police or blackmail us all. I wasn't sure which. Either way, it was one more reason to get the hell out of town.

Immediately.

"Now. I quit now." I crossed my arms. "I just wanted to tell you."

"What the hell, Sugar! You *and* that bitch Mila are both quitting? I count on you when the college kids all run home to mommy and daddy for the summer. Don't do this to me." He rubbed his temples. "Is this a coup of something? Did one of the kids leave a textbook you managed to understand and you two decided to extort a raise? Fine. Sold. I'll give you each a dollar raise per hour. Tell her, and both of you can get away with it this once."

I shook my head. He was a prick. I could understand the things they taught at school. I wasn't stupid. Neither was Mila. I didn't point any of that out. All I said was, "No. I just thought it was right to tell you in person."

For a moment, he stared at me. I didn't look away. I had a hell of a lot more to worry about than a pissed off coffee shop manager. He didn't intimidate me when he was my boss; he sure as fuck didn't intimidate me now. If he'd had video cameras, he'd have mentioned the murder by now—unless he hadn't seen them. I thought it was possible, but not likely.

"Don't think you can come back here for your paycheck, either. You or the other bitch. Just get out and stay out if this is how you're going to be," Jason snapped. His voice was louder and louder as he went.

I wanted to laugh at the ridiculousness of it all. I wasn't frightened, not of my penny-pinching boss. Drug dealers? Police? The man who punched me and stood over me with a holstered gun? Those all scared me. A grumpy ex-boss wasn't anywhere on my list.

"Sorry," I said.

"Go to hell," he replied, just as calmly.

I turned and left the back room. I didn't hurry. This was the last time I'd ever see this place. I'd worked there for over three years, and I was about to leave for good. There were customers I'd miss, and there were things about the familiarity of the shop that I'd miss. Just not enough to stick around and risk jail or death.

For a moment, I paused and scanned the ceiling, looking for anywhere that a camera could be hidden. There were a couple spots that were possibilities, but nothing I'd call likely. I was as sure as I could be that there wasn't a video of what happened. That was the best I could do.

Then I walked around the floor where the corpse had been, but other than that slight deviation, I walked straight to the door and out to the street. This was it. I was walking out of my job, abandoning my apartment, and leaving Rio Verde.

There was one stop I needed to make yet, one goodbye I needed to give, and then I'd go home and finish packing. Potential videos, witnesses who spilled our secret, dealers looking for cash and drugs . . . there was a growing list of reasons to get gone.

I DROVE over to Sinners Ink with something heavy in the pit of my stomach. Adam wasn't going to be as easy to leave as the rest of Rio Verde. We were friends. That was it.

He was Tommy's cousin.

He didn't do relationships.

I was too messed up to handle a real one anyhow.

None of those facts would meant that he'd think me taking off with Tommy was a great idea. He'd known Tommy and me during our days of throwing things at each other, screaming obscenities, and then screwing in the bathroom of some bar. He'd never quite reached the point of telling us that we were bad together, but he had been very encouraging when either of us mentioned breaking up for good.

This early, Sinners Ink was barely open. The light in the

window was on, and when I pushed on the door, it opened for me, but most of the shop lights were still off.

"Hello?" I called as I stepped inside.

The only sound was the *fwump* of the door closing behind me.

"Adam?" I walked farther into the waiting area.

A blue-haired girl with a lot of piercings came out of the back room. "Hey Sugar. What's up?"

"Is Adam in yet?" I asked.

"At his station," she said. "He'll be out to check his schedule in a few minutes or I can tell him you're here."

"I'll wait." I couldn't remember the girl's name. We'd been at parties together a few times, but I didn't really know her. I smiled to show I remembered her, though. "How are you?"

"Eh. You know how it is. Too much work, not enough play." She smiled. "I get my kicks by chasing out the bunnies when I can. It would be more fun, but Mr. Sex on A Stick won't let me use the broom to sweep them out. He lets them hang around, even though he's been bunny-free for a couple months now."

I raised both brows. "Really?"

"Oh yeah. You mustn't have seen him, or you'd have noticed. It's doing *great* things for his mood, too," she added sarcastically.

The idea of Adam being celibate was as likely as Tommy quitting drugs and smokes. I guess it was the season for a lot of changes. I shook my head. Adam hadn't seemed surly when I'd seen him.

"Oh," I said. I couldn't think of what else there was to say.

"If I didn't have to work with him, I'd give the boy a pity fuck. Can't screw where I work though. Boys get all clingy and turn into lost puppies, and then I'm left dealing with the guilt of kicking puppies."

I grinned, trying to picture six foot of muscle and ink being called a puppy. Maybe it would work if he was a Rottweiler or pit bull, but Adam didn't strike me as someone who'd ever be very puppy-ish. Sometimes I thought he had to have been born fully formed like one of those gods in myths. The idea of him as anything other than intense seemed too strange to consider.

Then Adam walked into the waiting area like he needed to appear to prove my point. He wasn't wearing anything fancy, just jeans and a black shirt. The jeans were well-fit without being tight, and the shirt was his usual, a t-shirt with a slogan. This one was from a shop called Naked Ink claiming: "instant sexy: just add ink." With him as an advertisement, I was betting people would buy into that theory pretty willingly.

All of his edges seemed to soften when he saw me. He smiled, arrived at the wrong conclusion about my appearance, and said, "Hey!"

"Hi." I felt awkward as he reached out—and I stepped back.

"Okay . . . What's up?"

I felt like a mountain of guilt had just fallen on me. "Adam," I started.

He turned away and said, "Betsy, what's my first appointment?"

Apparently, that was the blue-haired girl's name because she went over to the desk to get the appointment book.

"Adam!" I said louder. "I'm only here for a minute."

Betsey laughed, a husky sound that made me think she smoked far too much far too often, and asked, "Ooooh, are you here to help him with his prob—"

"Out, Bets." Adam cut her off and scowled. His already impressive biceps bulged as he crossed his arms. "Go check the stock or something."

"Seriously?" She laughed. "I'll go have a smoke. I'm not your errand girl."

"Actually, you are," he muttered.

She gave him the sort of indulgent smile I'd seen mothers give misbehaving children. "You keep thinking that, and I'll tell the bunnies you're pining after that special girl who shagged you after hours."

"Which one?" I asked, despite myself.

"Exactly," Betsey said with a smirk as she opened the door to the parking lot. "So many girls will suddenly think they're the one."

"Bitch," Adam muttered.

Betsey blew him a kiss and went outside.

"That girl's a menace." He shook his head. "She's been training, though, and once she's ready to work on her own, she's going to be amazing. Her art on paper is incredible already. It's different working on skin, but she's got the raw skills and the drive."

An unwelcome flare of jealousy filled me—and it was followed quickly by guilt. I had no right to care whether he thought Betsey was amazing. I had no rights at all where Adam was concerned, especially now that I was going to make things work with Tommy.

"What's up?" His words faded away suddenly. His gaze narrowed.

I squirmed. I knew how I looked. My face was bruised from what happened at work, and I realized belated that I was wearing one of Tommy's shirts. I watched Adam's friendly expression fade as he noticed.

Adam caught my hand in his. "Something you wanted to tell me, Sasha?"

I met his angry gaze and said, "Tommy and I talked last night."

He raised both brows. "I thought you said you weren't--"

"We're back together." I refused to look away.

"Are you a fucking serious?" Adam stared at me.

I nodded. "I'm sorry if I hurt you."

He laughed, but not like anything was funny. "What? One last hurrah before you went back to my *cousin?*"

I bowed my head. "I'm sorry, Adam."

He turned his back on me. "Is that it, Sasha? Sorry?"

"I know what I did was wrong but . . ."

He turned to stare at me. "Does he know where you spent the night?"

I shook my head. "No."

"Do you like how he hurts you?" He stepped closer. "Is that it? You like the fucking violence? The way he treated you?"

"Maybe." I shrugged. I couldn't defend myself. I couldn't tell him I was lying even more today, that I wasn't going to be with Tommy, that I just wanted to protect them both from the trouble I was in. If I told him, he'd do something stupid to try to protect me. That was who he was.

"What happens when he goes too far some night? The way you two fight is going to explode worse and worse." He touched my bruised face and his anger seemed to vanish. "I don't want that for either of you. I saw him last night, at The Blind Tiger. He chatted up some waitress after telling me how you'd come back to him. He left with her. Is that what you really want? A man who screws around, who hurts you, who gets you all fucked up on drugs? That's who he is."

I stepped backward. "What Tommy and I do is none of your business. I'm not yours."

He let out a sigh and muttered, "Whose fault is that?"

For a moment, I didn't know what to do or say. I just stared at him.

"Do you really think I didn't notice the way you look at me?" He stepped closer, backing me up against the counter where Betsey conveniently wasn't. "Do you know how easy it would be to *not* let my arm brush against you when I tattoo you? Do you think I'm like that with everyone?"

I stared at him, feeling thirteen kinds of stupid. I *had* thought that.

"I see you shiver when I touch you. It's no accident when I let my arm rest on you so the vibrations of the machine go into your body." He put a hand on either side of me, trapping me between his muscular arms. "It's the most unprofessional thing I've ever done, Sasha. The way I touch you when I work on your tattoo is not normal. . . . I can't help myself though. You looked like you were going to fall apart when I started tattooing your stomach, and I *wanted* you to. You don't belong with Tommy . . . and—"

Adam stepped closer, and then it wasn't just his arms keeping me in place. We were chest-to-chest, hip-to-hip.

"I thought you finally realized it." He leaned his forehead against mine and whispered, "Don't go back to him, Sasha. You're no good together. You know I'm right. Think about the dreams you said you had for the future. Do you see him giving you that little house and kids? Do you want to raise kids with a drug dealer?"

I took a steadying breath. I couldn't do this. Not to him. Not to Tommy. Not to myself. I felt like my already unstable nerves were about to shatter. "He *loves* me."

Adam's lips pressed together in a harsh line. I'd seen that look when he was about two minutes from a fight, but I'd never seen him look at *me* like that.

Silently, he stepped away from me.

I stumbled a little from the loss of his body against mine. I closed my eyes for a moment, attempting to find some sort of composure. The only plan I had was pretending the last few minutes hadn't happened, pretending that last night wasn't the single most emotional experience I'd had in my life.

I opened my eyes and stared at Adam as I announced, "Tommy and I are headed out of town for a while. If I give you my key, could you just . . . hold it?"

Adam walked over to the door, locked it, and flipped off the big neon sign that said OPEN. It was as close to a notice that I was in trouble as I was going to get. This wasn't the good sort of trouble either.

"Don't," I said.

He folded those beautiful arms over his chest, making the already big muscles bulge. "This is more than getting back with him. What happened that sent you to my bed last night, Sasha?"

"Nothing," I lied. "I had . . . an itch. I wanted to scratch it before I said yes to Tommy."

I wished I didn't have to lie, but a man was dead and I had a bunch of drug money now. Tommy was out turning the drugs into more money. The number of things that were crazy illegal was ridiculous. I didn't ask for any of it to happen. I'd rather the drugs and the money were in the live hands of the creep that came into The Coffee Cave, but that wasn't possible. I wasn't going to say I was sorry that Jess had shot that guy either. I still wasn't sure if he'd have shot *me*. At the very least, he'd have continued to beat me.

"You can talk to me," Adam said. "We're still friends, aren't we?"

I nodded. "I ruined that."

"Then make it right. Don't lie to me, Sash," he said in a gentle voice.

Even after the ugly things I had just said, even after I said I used him, he wanted to help me.

Adam deserved someone better than me. I'd ruin him.

I tried to look innocent, smiling up at Adam, eyes wide. "Everything's under control."

He shook his head. "Do you know when people say that? When shit is all fucked to hell and back. What did Tommy do now? And how did you get involved?"

"Nothing. He didn't do a thing." I sighed. "Just keep hold of my key, okay? I'll call you if I'm not coming back."

He put his hands on my arms and held me steady when I tried to walk to the door of the shop. "Let me help you, Sasha."

Stronger girls have bent under the intense stare that Adam was giving me. He knew he was gorgeous, and he was giving me those I-care-about-you eyes. I didn't even think he realized when he did it anymore. It was reflex. Like breathing.

"Come on, Sash," he whispered my name while staring into my eyes. "Just talk to me."

I felt like I was the only girl in the world when he looked at me that way and said my name. I wondered if he was well aware of how persuasive he could be. He always acted like he found all the bunny love confusing, but right now, I suddenly wanted to question everything I knew about Adam. How could he be unaware of the power he had over any woman with a pulse when he stared at them like that?

I was frozen under his gaze. He was too close, and I wanted to be a horrible person. It was all I could do to remind myself that Adam was forbidden . . . for so many reasons.

I wasn't ever going to join the ranks of ink bunnies that only got tattoos as a way to proposition him or the club girls who were all but giving him handjobs in the bar. There were a million girls in line to get their one night wrapped around his hard, sweaty body. I was just Girl Number Million-and-One.

"Sasha, please just think about what you're doing," Adam urged. He had begun to rub his hands up and down my arms.

I bit my lip to keep the whimper from escaping. It wasn't fair that he was touching me and looking at me like that now that I knew what we could be like together.

I stepped away, moving out of his reach. "I *have*. I'm leaving with Tommy. Just . . . just don't ask questions. He didn't do anything wrong. He's taking care of me, and everything will be *fine*."

He scowled, and his lips pressed together in a hard line. But he still held out his hand for my key.

I dropped my spare key into his palm. "Thank you."

All he did was nod. Then he walked over to the door and pushed it open. He didn't say a word as I walked past him. When I looked back, the sign lit up and said OPEN again, and Adam had disappeared inside Sinners Ink where I couldn't see him anymore.

ADAM

Adam watched Sasha walk away, a sight he was all too familiar with by now. Being patient for a girl wasn't something he'd ever done . . . not before her. Usually a smile and a once over look was all it took for a girl to agree to whatever he suggested. That was all he'd needed for the past decade. Sasha was special though. Yeah, he saw how she looked at him, but she listened to him too. She insisted on doing everything the hard way—no hand-outs, no leaning on anyone. Hell, she was determined to get up and fix dinner for *him* when he stopped by her place because she had the flu. The girl was fierce. If he'd met her before she met Tommy, he might have considered setting down real roots for a change.

"Sugar's the problem then?" a voice asked.

He turned and found Betsey standing in the shop, looking like she was ready to offer him a hug and a pat on the head.

"The bunny deterrent? You're hung up on her, and that's why you're on this chastity kick, right?" Betsey clarified when Adam didn't reply.

"Sasha's a friend."

Betsey snorted. "*I'm* a friend, so are Alamo, Chelsea, and

Viking Mike. You don't pin any of them to the counter. I've seen all sorts of nonsense, Adam, but that's the first time I had to walk out of the room here. You two looked like you were ready to ignite."

"Leave it alone, Bets."

She held her hands up in surrender. "I'm just saying you need to either fuck her or find an outlet because you're a bitch lately. It's like you've got man-PMS and went on a crash diet at the same time."

"Man-PMS?"

She waved her hand like she was brushing it away. "The *point*, my dear bunny-bait, is that something tells me that you haven't ever been pussy-free since . . . you were old enough to want it." She looked at him slowly from boot to hair, and then she shook her head and grinned. "Like I told Sugar, I don't fuck where I work, but if I did, I'd be here to help you with your problem. I'm not, and if she's not either, you need to get some from one of the willing thumpers."

Adam closed his eyes and willed himself not to snarl at her. Betsey was trying to be a friend. There was nothing she was saying that was untrue either. He'd just spent the past several months working to get closer to Sasha, avoiding his usual casual encounters. He thought that would show her that she mattered. He'd been patient, not rushing her, but not getting caught up in anything else.

Then finally got together, and he was sure everything would be on track finally--and now she was back with Tommy.

"Fuck it," Adam muttered. "When's my first appointment?"

Betsey looked at the book. "Three."

"Call Mike. See if he can come in early."

"Are you taking the day off?"

Ignoring her question, Adam walked back to his station. He wasn't going to tell the office manager/tattooist in training that he was walking out to get his dick wet and attitude improved. She knew far too much as it was.

Once he heard that Mike was on his way, Adam called Ella. "You free for an hour or two? It's Adam."

"I can be."

"Meet me at my place in thirty minutes."

She laughed. "Definitely."

Adam disconnected and looked up to see his reflection in the mirror. This was who he was. He was a fool to try to change.

There weren't any appointments, and Mike was less than twenty minutes from arriving when Adam walked out. Betsey, smartly, said nothing as he passed her.

His one concession to bad decisions was foregoing a helmet. Arizona allowed riders to decide for themselves if they were over eighteen. It was stupid. He'd heard plenty about guys dying in accidents, but he needed to keep a few vices. Women and his Super Glide Harley Davidson were the two he couldn't give up. He straddled his bike and headed toward the one-room studio apartment he'd called home the past few years. It wasn't much, but he didn't need much. He wasn't staying in Rio Verde forever. It was just a stop along the road. All he needed was a rental garage to store his Explorer and bike trailer, a small apartment to store his few things, and some cash for food, rent, and a gym membership since hauling his own weights around was impractical. He didn't want to be tied down with things.

The ride to his apartment was too short for his mood, but hopefully Ella would remove some of his stress. Three months without sex had been hell on his mood. The only times he'd felt good lately were when he had worked out hard enough that he was exhausted or when he saw Sasha.

He'd thought it was worth it.

He'd thought she was worth it.

And she just went back to Tommy.

Adam didn't even speak to Ella when he saw her waiting at his door. He poured all of his pent-up frustration and need into a kiss that had her wrapping both legs around him.

When he paused to unlock the door, she nipped his throat and said, "Nice to see you, too."

He laughed. Ella was reliable. She wasn't looking for promises like so many of the girls who came around the shop. She was a friend of sorts. They didn't talk much, but they didn't have any lies or expectations either.

Once inside the apartment, she lowered her feet to the floor and stepped back to give him an appraising look.

He pulled his t-shirt off and tossed it aside.

"I've missed this," she said as she stripped.

He didn't reply. He wasn't sure if he *had* missed it. He certainly missed getting off. But casual sex? He wasn't sure he'd missed that part.

He unbuttoned his jeans and shoved them down.

"I missed *that* too," she murmured in a cheeky voice as she lowered her eyes to his cock.

Then Ella was kissing and stroking and nipping him all over. She murmured the usual flattering things. It should have excited him, but his mind wasn't any more cooperative that his body.

Adam wasn't stupid. He knew exactly how he looked, and he'd been using it to his advantage since he was a teenager. That was when he realized that working out equated to getting laid. It was a fucking epiphany, like the angels sang and light shined down from heaven, when he realized it was really that easy. He hit the weights hard the summer before his sophomore year of high school, and by the time school rolled around that year, Adam discovered that there were a whole list of girls who now looked at him like he was something new. By Halloween, he'd discovered that some of those girls—older ones mostly—were willing to teach him what they liked. He learned where and how to touch them. More importantly, he learned that as long as they got off first and often, they'd be willing to do just about anything.

Ella was on her knees in front of him now.

He groaned as her mouth closed over him. *This*, he had missed. All of his worries and responsibilities vanished when he was naked with someone equally desperate to chase bliss.

But then he made the mistake of looking down at her, of grabbing her hair in his hands. Ella was a tiny, curvy, little thing with long blonde hair. She was also gifted in blow jobs. What she wasn't was Sasha.

He pushed Ella away and led her over to his bed.

Shoving thoughts of Sasha out of his mind, he focused on the girl in his arms.

Several times, she tried to move so she could fuck him. He gently shoved her back and kissed her instead.

He caught her frown the second time and saw her open her mouth to speak, so he kissed her thoroughly so she didn't ask questions he couldn't answer.

It was ridiculous, but he couldn't do it. Fucking someone because he was pissed at Sasha wasn't a good idea. His body objected painfully to that realization, but he wasn't going to be a slave to his needs.

"Are you okay?" Ella whispered.

He didn't answer that either. He was horny, frustrated, and angry. Definitely *not* okay.

He'd called Ella here though, and he'd never walked away from a girl or woman who wasn't smiling. That was the number one lesson he'd learned as a teenager: Always satisfy your partner. He wasn't about to fail on that.

"Come here, doll." Adam pulled her up and flipped her onto her back.

He saw the gleam in Ella's eyes. He might not be able to fuck her, but that didn't mean she was going to leave without at least one orgasm. She wasn't to blame for his unwillingness to fuck. That was all him.

"No scratching," he reminded her.

Adam wasn't going to let Sasha see him with scratches on his shoulders or arms. He didn't owe her anything. She'd made that clear. *Hell,* he thought, *I probably won't even see her again. She'd never know.*

But I would.

Even after she'd used him and tossed him aside, he wanted to be worthy of her.

As Ella writhed under Adam's tongue and hands, he imagined Sasha. Again. Thinking of her was all it took to make him so hard he thought he could come without a single thrust. He pretended it was Sasha under his tongue, and he wanted *her* to scream in pleasure. He wanted her to know that no one, especially his jackass cousin, could make her happier than he could.

He pushed Ella's legs wider apart and tugged her to the edge of the bed. He slid to the floor, kneeling so that he had only thigh and pussy in his sight. Then he went to work with the sort of dedication that made women beg him not to stop. Not that he would. Having a woman fall apart from his touch was like a gift.

"Fuck yes!"

Ella's voice ruined his fantasy, but Adam didn't stop, pushing her toward a second orgasm. Once she was whimpering and limp, he slid up her body and looked at her. There was something almost holy about the way a woman looked after she came apart. He didn't understand a lot of philosophy or theology, but he knew pure beauty when he saw it.

Ella was there, willing and radiant in her pleasure, but she wasn't the one he wanted. She didn't smell like Sasha or sound like her. Adam stood and then sat on the edge of the bed. She moved over to make room for him.

Quietly, he told Ella, "I can't do this. I'm sorry."

For a moment, she was silent, appraising him.

"Love's a bitch, isn't it?" she whispered.

Adam laughed bitterly.

"I hope she knows how lucky she is," Ella added.

And Adam couldn't even speak. He got up, got dressed, and went to see his cousin.

SUGAR

Tommy didn't show up or call that night, and I was starting to jump at every noise. I didn't go back to The Coffee Cave. I did go over to Tommy's place, but he wasn't there. Or if he was, he wasn't answering the door.

I didn't want to believe he'd ditched me. I also didn't want to believe he was in trouble. It had to be one of the two though.

I debated just taking off, but decided to give him one more day. If he didn't turn up by Wednesday, I was going to write off the money from the coke and hit the road.

Adam had called to ask if I was okay, but I didn't call back. I texted a quick note to him. That was all I could handle. Tommy was late, and I wasn't sure I could pretend that Adam hadn't rocked my world. I couldn't be sure I could lie to Adam—on top of the murder and theft, and oh yeah, trying to run away with a man I didn't actually love.

On Tuesday, I thought about stopping by Sinners Ink to see if Adam knew anything, but I couldn't. I wasn't going to put myself in temptation's path unless it was impossible to avoid. I was scared and alone, and if Adam looked at me like he had the other morning, I couldn't guarantee that I wouldn't crack.

I *wanted* to tell Adam everything. . . . so I stayed away from Sinners Ink. I stayed away from most everywhere. I went out and bought a third and forth suitcase, and I got a few moving boxes for my stuff. I spent the first day packing my place, and I spent the morning of the second toting it to a storage center I'd rented. Even if Tommy didn't come back with the money, I still had more than enough to get out of Rio Verde. There was over two hundred thousand dollars in my apartment. If I was careful, I could get a job to live off and use the stolen money to make sure I'd be okay even if the job was lower paying than the sort of job I usually had to get. Not giving any notice at The Coffee Cave meant I had a hole in my work record, but I didn't want anyone in wherever I ended up to tie me back to The Coffee Cave.

Then midday Wednesday, I got a call. It wasn't Tommy, though.

"Sasha? It's Adam."

I couldn't speak. I felt horrible dread at the sound of his voice. There was something wrong. I knew it. I tried to push those thoughts away. I told myself he was probably just calling because of what happened between us.

"Are you home?" he said.

"Yeah," I whispered.

"Open your door."

I was glad that he hadn't let himself in with the key I'd given him, but I wasn't sure how I felt about Adam in my apartment. I walked over and unlocked my door, and when I saw him there, he lowered the phone he had held to his ear.

"Can I come in?" He looked at me, and I *knew*. I knew I wasn't wrong. Something had happened.

I nodded and lowered my phone. Then I stepped back to let him inside. He'd been here before, but usually only with Tommy. The only exception was that one weekend when I was sick. He'd brought me soup then.

Adam closed the door behind him—and then he locked it.

I stared at him for a moment. "Why did you lock that?"

"Let's sit down." He put his hand in the middle of my back, and he led me to my sofa.

Any lingering doubts I had that things were bad had vanished. "You're scaring me."

"I'm sorry," he said. He motioned to the sofa.

I sat.

He sat next to me. "I don't know how to say this . . ."

"Just say it." I squeezed my hands together so tightly that they hurt.

"Tommy had my name and number on him. That's why they called me. Yours wasn't there. I'm glad. It was . . . better that you didn't have to go." Adam shook his head, like he was shaking away the words, and then he reached out and grabbed my hands. He unfolded them and took one in his. "Sash, Tommy's dead."

I stared at him.

I blinked.

I swallowed. Opened my mouth. Closed it. I shook my head. This couldn't be happening.

But Adam kept talking: "I went down and identified him. They already knew because of his wallet, but . . . they still needed me to come and . . . identify him."

"He *can't* be dead. It's a mistake." I tried to pull my hand out of Adam's, but he didn't let me go. "No."

"There's no mistake, Sasha. I saw him." Adam squeezed my hand. "I'm sorry. I know you thought he wasn't in trouble, but—"

"*He* wasn't the one in trouble."

It hit me then, like someone had punched me in the stomach. The awful truth made me feel like puking. Tommy was dead because of me. Whether it was because he was trying to sell the coke I gave him or because they realized where the coke came from, it was my fault.

"You need to go," I blurted out. "It's not safe to be around me. They'll kill you too." I used our clasped hands, since he still held mine, to try to pull him, but Adam Bradbery was a wall of muscle. I couldn't budge him at all.

"I'm not going anywhere without you," he said.

"You aren't listening, Adam! They *killed* Tommy. You need to get out of here before someone realizes that you were here. You can't be near me." My voice was bordering on shrill, but I couldn't stop it.

"No."

"Don't be stupid!" I jerked my hand out of Adam's grasp. "I need to get into his place to see if he left . . . anything there. You need to go. Just leave."

He grabbed me as I tried to stand up. "We can stop at his place if you really want, but you're not staying here *or* going there alone."

I couldn't pull away from him, so I didn't even try this time. I twisted so I was facing him. "I'm *not* staying here. After I check if he left anything at the apartment, I'm going to get out of Rio Verde. I told you I was leaving. I was just waiting on—" I cut myself off and shook my head before I could continue. "You just stay away from here and from his place and . . . just stay away from anything about us. That's the only safe—"

"No," he interrupted. "I'm staying with you, Sash. Wherever you are is where I'll be."

When I didn't say anything, Adam wrapped his arms around me and held me. I let him. Three days ago, I was worried that a stranger was going to kill me. Three days ago, I was an accomplice in hiding a murder and stealing from the dead. I hadn't meant for any of that to happen, but it had. I thought the money was a chance for a future, a chance to start over somewhere else. Now Tommy was dead. I couldn't let anything happen to Adam too.

"We'll get this sorted out," he said.

I pushed myself out of his arms and whispered, "It's my fault, Adam. I need to get out of town. Now. You can't be seen with me."

Adam ignored what I said. He just kept on with his plan as if I hadn't spoken. "I'll drive you to Tommy's place, and then we'll come back here and load up whatever you need." He stared into my eyes and said, "I'm coming with you wherever you're going."

There was no other way to make him understand that he couldn't be around me. I knew he hated drugs. I had to tell him the truth—or as much of it as I could. I didn't look away as I confessed, "I came across some money and two kilos of cocaine. Tommy was selling it for me. I doubt there's any money or coke at his place, but even without that, I have plenty. I don't need you to take care of me. Tommy tried. He's dead now. He's dead *because of me.*"

I wanted to curl up and cry about that, but I couldn't. I needed to stay strong until I was far away from here. Then I could fall apart. Not now. I sat down again though. I might be able to hold off on the tears, but I felt like grief and fear were stealing my strength.

Adam came to crouch in front of me. "Tommy's the one who got you started on drugs. Not the other way around. You've only known him a couple of years, but I *know* my cousin. He was mixed up with all sorts of stupid shit for as long as I can remember. That's why I came to Rio Verde, to check on him for my Aunt Grace."

Adam looked away for a moment, and I figured he had to be thinking about his family. I didn't ask. I couldn't yet. I'd never met any of them other than Adam. I wasn't sure if Tommy had even told them about me.

After a moment, Adam cleared his throat and continued, "If it wasn't this, it would've been something else. We all knew it. If not for Aunt Grace's constant badgering of God, I'm pretty sure Tommy would've been in jail or dead years ago. That woman prays so much, I think God's probably been afraid to tell her no, but even all of her prayers could only buy him so much time."

"You should go home," I said. "There will be a funeral, and—"

"*No*. I already told them I had to handle some things because of how he died. They didn't ask, but they know I won't be home with the body." Adam paused again. "I said my goodbyes to him. Now, I'm going to get you out of here. I just need to grab some clothes and my work stuff, and then we'll get you packed—"

"I've been packed for two days," I interrupted.

"Good. That makes it quicker." He stood and pulled me to my feet. "If you want, I can go over to Tommy's place to look around on my own."

"No." I stepped around Adam and grabbed my purse. "Let's go."

Downstairs in the lot, we both pulled out our keys.

Adam frowned. "I don't think you should drive."

Even though I wanted to argue, I knew he was right. There weren't a lot of people on the road, but there were enough that I wasn't going to endanger them to try to prove that I was calmer than I really was. I dropped my keys back into my purse. "Fine."

"Are you okay on the bike or do you want me to drive your car?"

"Bike."

Adam motioned me toward his Harley. It wasn't a chopped-out beast with ape hangers, unusual tires, or an overload of chrome. It was a classy looking, solid machine with a silver dragon detailed on the body and matte finish pipes. Those pipes were just this side of legal, and I'd listened to Adam's Harley growl enough times that I was almost smiling at the thought of being on it. It was a beautiful bike.

"Just hold on and follow my body when I lean," he ordered as he straddled the bike.

My body thrilled at being so close to him, so I let myself lean against him.

"You're safe," he assured me.

I didn't tell him I knew I didn't need to cling to him, or that his wasn't the first bike I'd been on. I didn't mention that I'd spent a few months with the sort of guys who thought Harleys meant that if you weren't their "old lady" you needed to pay with "ass, gas, or grass." I just threw my leg over and settled in behind him on the tiny, uncomfortable seat that made it quite clear that there wasn't a woman who sat here regularly.

I thought back to the times I'd seen Adam out and about. I don't remember many girls being allowed on his bike at all. Under different circumstances, I'd feel special for being for on his Harley.

I knew that he didn't carry a helmet, so I didn't bother asking for one. Riding without it was far from the most dangerous thing I'd done that week. Pressing my chest up against Adam's back and wrapping my arms around him was more dangerous than the lack of helmet—probably for both of us. I closed my eyes as he started the bike and rested my face against the back of his shoulder. Riding together was somewhere between dancing and sex. Two bodies had to move like one. The minute adjustments, the speed, the vibration of the engine and wheels churning over the road all combined to create a sort of symbiosis that few other experiences could.

I lost myself in the feel of it.

Too soon, however, we were stopping. Worse yet, I was walking into a building I'd really rather not enter today . . . or ever again. It felt wrong to be there with Adam. It felt even worse to realize that since Tommy walked out of his apartment on Sunday, the only times I'd smiled were thanks to Adam.

I pushed away that guilt-inducing thought and walked toward the building. Adam was at my side. I noticed him scanning the area, but he didn't stop me from opening the door to the stairwell.

When we reached Tommy's apartment, I lifted my hand to knock before I remembered that he wasn't there. He'd never be there again. Tommy was dead, and it was my fault. If I hadn't taken the coke, he'd be alive. If I hadn't brought it to him, he'd be alive. If I hadn't gone to work that night, he'd be alive. There were a million things I could've decided differently, and he'd still be alive.

"Do you still have a key?" Adam asked, startling me a little.

I wasn't sure how long I'd stood there motionless.

I shook my head. Tommy and I had fought over that damn key more times than I could count. Sometimes we'd fought because he thought I should keep it because it was my home too, and sometimes we fought because he thought I shouldn't have it in case he was with someone else.

Adam reached into his pocket and pulled out what looked like a pocket knife, except that when he opened it, it wasn't blades that extended. This was a multi-tool of lock picks.

"I'm not going to ask," I said.

"Good idea."

After a couple moments, Adam unlocked the door, and we went inside the apartment.

I was pretty sure that Tommy had to have had either the drugs or any money he got for them with him when he was killed, but I still had to check. Anything he had left of either would be here. "Start in the kitchen," I said. "Check all the boxes in the cupboard too."

"I know the drill for finding a stash of money or drugs," Adam said. "Freezer, pantry, and cupboards."

"Right," I said, and I had to wonder what all I didn't know

about him. Most people didn't think to look inside food for a stash unless they'd lived in Tommy's world for a while. Adam wasn't straight-edge or anything, but the hardest things he imbibed were whiskey and gin. No cigarettes or drugs. He didn't smoke *anything*. The only needles he'd touched, as far as I knew, were tattoo needles. Maybe someday, I'd ask Adam how he knew where all to look.

"I'll take the bedroom and bathroom while you do the kitchen."

"Check inside the TP holder," he called as I walked away.

Yeah, he knew far too much. There were secrets there. Maybe those secrets explained why he stayed to keep an eye on Tommy or why he was so proud of me for getting clean.

I walked into Tommy's bedroom . . . and stopped. I felt like I'd been punched in the gut. Just a couple of days ago, we were talking about a chance at a real future.

I didn't cry. I couldn't. I *wouldn't*.

Maybe it was stupid, but I grabbed one of Tommy's shirts from the floor and smelled it. Before I could think too long on it, I scooped a few more of his shirts and shoved them into a duffle bag. Then I started going through all of the drawers, the laundry basket up against the wall, and the pockets of his jacket. I felt underneath the dresser for anything taped there, and I did the same for the bed and the closet shelf. I knew that some of these places were too small for the amount of cash or drugs I was hoping to find, but maybe there would be a key or a note. Tommy and I had both hidden things in the apartment before, mostly when I was looking for drugs he wouldn't give me.

By the time I'd searched the entire bedroom, I'd found no trace of drugs or money. I grabbed a few pictures of us, a necklace he'd bought me that I'd thrown at him in one of our uglier fights, and a few more pieces of clothing—mine this time. I tossed it all into a duffle bag.

Then I went to the living room to search there.

It was stupid, I guess, but kneeling on the floor near the coffee table and sofa to look under the sofa was what did it. I finally started crying. It wasn't we romantic or anything last I saw him, but it was where our last night together and he'd been a friend.

I was gasping in grief a few moments later when I felt strong arms wrap around me.

Quickly I jerked away. "Don't," I said. "Just don't touch me."

Adam didn't say anything. He just lifted the sofa cushions and checked under them. He didn't put them back down, but moved on to the next thing. I looked toward the kitchen and saw that it was all out of order too. The whole place was starting to look like there had been a shakedown, and I guess there sort of had been.

"Are you ready to get out of here?" Adam said, breaking into my thoughts.

I turned to see Adam standing beside me. He looked about as comfortable as I felt. I knew he and Tommy had their share of differences of opinions, but they'd been family, *and* Adam had had to identify the body. All of that was after he'd asked me to leave Tommy. I couldn't imagine how awful today had been for Adam.

"I'm sorry," I said.

"For . . . ?"

"You're probably upset too, and you're having to deal with my shit." I closed the drawer.

Adam laughed, not in amusement but bitterly. "Sweetheart, I've been cleaning up after Tommy since we were still in middle school. It's been what I do for so long that it's not even worth mentioning."

I opened my mouth, thought better of the things I wanted to say, and closed it. It hit me with a disturbing amount of clarity that Adam had been looking after Tommy all along. He had told us both that we were bad together. I'd thought that he was trying to protect me too, but as I looked at him now, I changed my mind. How far was he willing to go to keep Tommy safer? Were the things he said to me at Sinners Ink about me at all? I wasn't ugly. I wasn't a model or anything, but I was pretty and my body was enough to make people look more than once.

Adam must have thought Tommy had started hitting me, and he was trying to keep Tommy out of jail for assault, I thought.

He'd come to Rio Verde to protect Tommy, and I guess that somewhere along the line, Adam had decided that part of that was to keep me away from Tommy. I had thought that he cared, that we were friends. I was a fool. It was ridiculous to think that someone as wonderful as Adam would want to be more.

We hooked up because I'd thrown myself at him. That was all it was. I was suddenly extra grateful that I'd stepped away from him instead of believing it could be real.

It was just lust.

Unfortunately, that lust was a lot harder to manage a few minutes later when I was straddling him on the back of his Harley again. I couldn't not hold on to him. I mean, technically, I could. Riding on the back of a bike isn't really like in the movies where you have to cling to the man in front of you like a desperate monkey. When I rode with the guy I'd dated a few years ago, I learned that I could lean back without feeling unsafe. The truth was, though, that I wanted to feel close to someone right now. Being pressed up against Adam made things seem less overwhelming.

. . . except for the lust. I was a simply going to have to ignore that like I had been doing. I had months of practice, well over a year if I was completely honest with myself. I slipped up once, but Adam wouldn't touch me again after the things I'd said.

I was both relieved and disappointed a little while later when we stopped by a garage where Adam's dark green Ford Explorer and tow-behind bike trailer were stored.

Although I was surprised to see Adam with anything other than his Harley, I guess it made sense for someone who didn't live in one area forever. He'd taken several trips to work to other shops in other states during the time I'd known him. Having a larger vehicle was only logical.

"Can you drive the Explorer to the shop or are you too shaky?"

I gave him a look that was probably ruder than it should've been. It was a valid question. I'd been sobbing. Tommy was dead. It wasn't like I was in prime condition to drive. I needed to get it together though. Things weren't going to get easier right now, and I couldn't expect someone else to do everything for me. I never had before, and I wasn't going to start today.

"Sure," I said. "I'm good."

Adam looked skeptical, but it was either leave the bike behind or go with this plan. "You're sure?"

"I'll go slow," I added. "Honestly, Adam. I can handle this. I could go on my own."

"No." He shook his head at me, but said nothing else.

When we got to Sinners Ink, I waited outside while Adam went in for his work gear and, presumably, quit. He didn't say anything when he opened the back door of the Explorer to put a box of his things inside.

I followed him to his apartment building, parked, and went inside. He offered me a drink, and asked if I could pack a cooler with anything worth saving from the fridge. I did that, and packed a few things from the cupboards, and tossed the rest of the contents of the fridge. I'd done the same thing at my place earlier in the week. Then, I sat quietly on his sofa while he packed. By the time we had gathered up, I felt like the whole world was in a big cloud of gauze. Everything felt hazy around me.

I told Adam as much when we were loading his things in the

back of his Explorer with the small bag of stuff I'd packed at Tommy's place.

"Shock." Adam said as he slammed the back of his Explorer closed.

I startled at the sound of it closing, and then I followed him to the side of the Explorer. Belatedly I realized that he was going to the passenger door, but I understood why a moment later. He opened the door for me, which wasn't totally weird but *felt* like it was just then. Everything felt wrong.

"There was a guy hassling me at The Cave, and someone shot him," I said. I didn't get in the Explorer yet. I wasn't sure why I was telling Adam when I hadn't told Tommy. Maybe I was telling him *because* I hadn't told Tommy. Now Tommy was dead. I was headed out of town. Adam deserved to know.

Instead of any sort of judgmental reaction, Adam just nodded. "That's where you found the drugs."

"And money. A lot of it," I added. "I gave the coke to Tommy, and he was going to sell it and add that to the money I have and we were going to both start over."

"Okay," he said. "Now, get in. I need to hitch the trailer."

I stared at Adam. I'd just told him about a murder, illegal money, and drugs—and he told me he needed to hitch his bike trailer. Even though I'd mentioned the coke and cash before, the whole murder thing was new. Maybe he didn't hear me right. I said, a little louder this time, "A man is dead. He was trying to hurt me, but . . . still, he'd dead. He was killed."

Adam looked me straight in the eyes and asked, "Did you kill him?"

"No."

"Okay." Adam put his hand on my low back and gently pushed me toward the Explorer. "Get in the truck, Sasha."

I slid inside, and he closed the door.

A few minutes later, the bike trailer was hitched up. If not for our bags, we could take off on the Harley that was now parked and tied down on the trailer. I'd never ridden with Adam before today, but I'd already known that I liked it. The summer after I graduated high school, I'd dated a guy who was a couple years older than me who had an old Triumph he'd restored. There were a few others after him. There was something altogether perfect about the freedom of a motorcycle and open road. It was even better with a Harley and Adam. Briefly, I considered suggesting we ditch the SUV and set out on the bike, but I couldn't ride solo and wherever we went, it would be useful to have a vehicle I could drive too. I was already counting on Adam far too much.

When he got into the driver's side and started the Explorer, he didn't say a thing.

"I'd understand if you wanted to bail," I said. "I can take my car, and you can stay here."

He was silent for about two blocks and then he said, "Either someone knows about the cash and coke and tied it to Tommy, or this was because of something else he got himself into."

"It was my fault," I started.

Adam held up his hand in a halting gesture. "The only way to know for sure why someone shot Tommy is to find the killer and ask. We're not doing that, so we don't know for sure why Tommy's dead now. It *is* a safe bet that it's because of the drugs, cash, or murder at the shop—but there are enough other things he's done that it might not be. Either way, it's best that we get out of town."

"I'm dangerous to be around right now. If they find me, they'll probably kill you too."

"They won't find either of us. Your car is still here, and you don't need to get a job that requires any paperwork. No one's going to think I have anything to do with it since everyone knows I'm not stupid enough to get caught up in drugs these days. I can keep you safe and hide you. I've lived without a trail before, Sash. If you went without me, they *would* find you, but it's not as likely if I'm with you. I know how to hide. Trust me."

I shuddered at the renewed thought of a killer trying to track me down. Later, I wanted to ask about the rest of what he'd just said, but for now, I didn't think I could handle knowing anything else. I kept my mouth firmly shut and shoved my questions far away for now.

Adam glanced over at me. "Call whoever you need to, and then we pull the card out of that phone."

I wasn't sure if the killer could find me through my friends or my phone, but I wasn't chancing it. I had told Mila she could keep in touch, but that wasn't going to work after all. Not now that Tommy was dead. I called Mila quickly, and after a brief hello, I told her, "Tommy's dead. I gave him the coke we found, and that was the last I saw him."

"Shit, Sugar! Are you okay? Where are you? Where are you going?"

I closed my eyes. She was my friend, as much as anyone in Rio Verde was, but I had an awful moment where I didn't trust her. I wasn't sure who I could trust. I didn't have any really close friends, just people I knew through work or through Tommy. I didn't have a family. I could vanish and no one would even notice or care. Tommy would've, but he was dead.

I decided not to tell Mila anything.

"In a car," I said. "I'm not sure where I'm going."

That wasn't a *complete* lie, but it wasn't all the way true either. I didn't mention that I was with Adam or tell her that I was still in Rio Verde. In my gut, I thought I could trust her, but tens of thousands of dollars was a great motive for all sorts of bad deci-sions. I had to wonder if someone else at The Coffee Cave that night wanted the coke, but hadn't said. I knew Mila wouldn't, and I was pretty sure that Ian wouldn't either, but there were enough people there that I didn't really know . . . and any of them could've talked to someone else.

After another couple minutes, I said, "Be safe, Mila. Tell Ian to be careful too if you talk to them."

"I will."

And that was it. I disconnected, and then I pried my phone open, pulled the SIM card out of my phone, and shoved it in my bag.

SUGAR

I wasn't sure where we headed, and I'm fairly certain Adam wasn't either. I wasn't ever intending on staying in Rio Verde, but my heart still clenched at leaving it. I liked to *choose* when I was going to leave town, not go running out with my tail tucked between my legs and two dead bodies behind me.

Although I hadn't actually *killed* the guy in the coffee shop or Tommy, I still felt guilty over their deaths. The creep was dead because he threatened me. Tommy was dead because he tried to protect me. I glanced over at Adam. I didn't want anything to happen to him too.

"You're staring, Sasha. Are you going to say something?"

"I'm sorry."

"For?"

"Tommy. Or maybe because you're in danger. Or because I thought . . ." My words faded.

"You thought?"

"I thought that I was leaving, so I let myself think there was no consequence," I said quietly.

"To using me?" He sounded harsh.

But I couldn't say I didn't deserve it. There were a lot of

stupid things I'd done in my life, but hurting Adam was high on my list. The best I could say was "I didn't mean to hurt you."

He nodded, and I was relieved that he didn't try to tell me that it wasn't my fault or that it was okay or any of those empty things people say. Adam might have shocked me lately, but he was still the guy I considered a friend. I felt foolish that I'd thought he wanted me for more, and the memory of us naked made me flush from head to toe.

I wasn't sure I could handle being around him if I thought there was any chance of a repeat event.

It was just sex.

The truth was that my coping mechanisms weren't healthy ones. That had been one of the glues that held me to Tommy: he would let me lose myself when I was hurt, and even when he was the one upsetting me, he was where I'd found the things that I'd needed to drown my pain. Whether it was the drugs or sex, he was my go-to for a fix. I didn't know how to fix the ache inside me without him to help me—and using Adam wasn't an option.

Because I want more than sex from him.

That was not going to happen. Ever.

"There's a shop out towards Joshua Tree where I can work for at least a week or two," Adam said, sounding like my friend despite everything. "It's not going to be too busy since we're moving into summer, but it won't be deserted yet."

I nodded.

"We can head out towards the coast after that or go north," Adam continued.

"Tommy and I didn't have a plan yet," I told him. "We were just going to go. I wanted a normal life."

Adam sighed. "Sasha, don't take his wrong, but—"

"When people say that, it means they're going to make an asshole comment," I interrupted.

"Right . . . so my 'asshole comment' is that you and Tommy

wouldn't have made things work. I've known—*knew* him for my whole life. Do you really think this is the first time he said he'd change?"

I knew he was right, and this was when I ought to have told him that I didn't really even get back with Tommy. Instead, I said, "He loved me."

"He did." Adam glanced over at me.

I could see him out of the corner of my eye, but I refused to look his way.

Adam continued, "I honestly think he loved you more than he's loved anyone in his life, but love doesn't change who you *are*. Tommy was a disaster headed towards destruction for *years* now. That wasn't going to change because he fell for an amazing girl."

"We might've made it work," I argued, just on principle. "I have plenty of money. We could've been normal, a little house, and maybe a baby some day."

"And you don't think he'd have wanted to use that money on some scheme? Invest it in some scheme 'just one more time'? He was my fucking family, Sasha. I've been the one who gave him the money to change his life, and you know what he did with it? He bought drugs. He 'invested' in stolen shit to resell it. He liked the rush of the scams and the deals." Adam sounded tired, like he was worn out by the things he was telling me. "He wasn't ever addicted to the drugs; they were a means to any end. He couldn't give up the schemes though."

"We'll never know if he could have," I said. I reached over and turned up whatever radio station Adam had on, and then I turned my attention to the desolate world outside the window. I didn't want to hear any of the things he was saying. They were versions of things Mila had said, ones Adam had said more kindly in the past . . . hell, strangers at parties had said some of them.

I knew Tommy wasn't a prince, but he loved me. No one else

had done that in my life. Sometimes, I thought my parents loved me, but I wasn't ever quite sure.

Adam wasn't even saying anything I hadn't thought myself, and I knew that my suggestion of leaving with Tommy wasn't the same as getting back together with him, but admitting that felt like betraying Tommy.

Everything in my life had fallen to pieces when the drug dealer walked into The Coffee Cave. There was nothing solid in my life. I had no job, no apartment, no boyfriend. No one loved me. No one would care that I'd vanish—except maybe people who wanted to hurt me.

The possibility that I could've saved Tommy was all I had left. I wasn't surrendering it just now.

WHEN ADAM PULLED into the tiny town of Joshua Tree, I was surprised. It wasn't that I expected a city the size of Rio Verde, but I expected something . . . I don't know, *bigger*. Maybe there would be more to see later, but so far it looked miniscule.

"I know a guy who can hook us up on a place," Adam said as he parked in front of a row of shops. "Wait here."

I didn't have any pressing need to argue, not right now. Later, I'd have to figure out what I was going to do in town, but today I just sort of wanted to hide. It seemed unreal that I'd been in Rio Verde that afternoon. Now I was in another state, in a town I'd never visited, alone with a man who made me crazy with feelings I didn't want.

There wasn't a lot to watch while I waited. I assumed we looked like any other couple on a vacation—not that there were a lot of tourists who rolled into desert towns in mid-May, but we didn't draw a lot of attention. That was good.

No more than twenty minutes passed before Adam was

sliding back into the driver's seat. He looked my way and asked, "Are you still doing okay?"

I nodded. All of my emotions felt too raw still. A nod was the best I could offer.

He handed a set of keys to me. "I rented a cabin a ways outside of town where it's more private. It's a vacation rental, pretty basic place, but there aren't any neighbors. I've used it before."

I nodded again.

Adam reached over briefly and squeezed my hand. "You're going to be okay, Sasha. We'll get you through this, and you'll be fine."

This time I couldn't nod. I didn't believe him. It seemed impossible that I could've left all the trouble behind.

"You could leave me here," I said quietly.

Adam stared at me like I was a fool, and then he said, "If they're coming, they'll come here eventually. Until they stop hunting you, I'm not leaving you alone."

I made a pained noise.

"They killed him, Sash. Murdered him. What are you doing to do if they come after you?"

I shrugged. It wasn't like I had a great plan. I just knew that I didn't want Adam to get hurt, too. I'd lied to him to piss him so he wouldn't come looking for me, but here he was, promising to keep me safe.

"That's my problem. Not yours."

Adam drove, not taking his eyes off the road while he did so. If it wasn't for the fear and guilt that filled me like a damned piñata about to burst open at the slightest tap, maybe I'd enjoy the scenery I was staring at out the window. As it was, I saw nothing but open space where monsters could spot us. We were exposed.

About ten minutes later, Adam parked in front of a tiny little house with a detached garage that looked almost as big as the house. It wasn't more than a one and half car garage, but the house was small too.

"It's not much," he said as we sat staring at the house.

The house was tucked into a slopping ravine, and until you were all but at the door you couldn't see it. Tiny and hidden.

I shot Adam a questioning look when I got out of the Explorer.

"It was the house with the garage or I park the bike in the main room," he said. "I rented this one last time because it was all Rudy had available. It's bigger than I need, but I liked that garage and I figured with both of us here . . ." His words drifted away as he went to the bike trailer and started untying his Harley.

"I'm going to take some things inside," I told him.

"I'll help in a minute," he muttered from where he stood beside the trailer.

I couldn't blame him. He wasn't the one who needed to get out of town, but there was a part of me that wanted to tell him that Harleys weren't the same as horses. He didn't need to feed it or brush it down before tending to human needs. I wasn't sure it would do any good though. He had next to no possessions. Most of what he had seemed fairly disposable. That bike was his one exception.

Inside the house, I stopped and looked around. It was a very sparse place. A bright red sofa was pushed up against one wall. Diagonal from it was a rocking chair with a blanket folded and draped over the arm. On the other side of the room was a small table with two chairs. A compact kitchen was visible from the doorway too. I walked farther into the house. Two doors opened off the main room. A cursory glance showed that one was a bedroom and the other a bathroom. The whole place seemed to be only those three rooms.

Three rooms.

I was going to live in the desert in a three-room house with Adam. How in the name of all that was holy was I supposed to do that? I shook my head.

Three rooms. One bedroom.

My first reaction should've been shock or fear or anger. It wasn't. I walked over to the bedroom to look closer. A double bed, night stand, and dresser were the whole of what was in there.

His room.

Where I shall not sleep or be when he is naked or near naked or awake or . . . Self-control was going to be a challenge.

I pushed my suitcase up against the wall in the living room. Then I went back out to the Explorer. This, at least, I could do.

I made several more trips while Adam moved the bike and trailer into the garage. I'd brought in my essentials, the bag of cash, and the groceries we'd carried from his place. I didn't make a big deal about the bag of cash. I wasn't exactly hiding it from Adam, but I didn't want to plop it on the floor and announce "look, stacks of money!" either. He hadn't asked how much cash, and I hadn't volunteered. It wasn't a *lie* because I said I'd taken cash, but an omission because I wasn't sharing unnecessary details.

When my hand came down on the bag of things from Tommy's place, I stopped. I couldn't handle that. I pushed it aside. There was a garage. It, and several boxes from my place, could go in there with the Harley.

"What else do you need?" Adam asked as he approached.

"Nothing." I stepped back. "Whatever you need. The rest can go in there." I gestured toward the garage, unable to meet his eyes.

He nodded. "I'll get my things."

Mutely, I turned back to the house.

He followed with two bags in hand. I went to the kitchen and began putting away groceries. Trying to sound casual, I said, "If I could have one drawer, that would be great."

Adam frowned. "I don't need any of them. It makes sense for you to take them since you'll have the bed."

"I can take the sofa." I met his eyes briefly. "I'm smaller."

"It's a pull-out bed, Sasha. Take the bedroom." He didn't phrase it like there was any room for discussion.

"If you, um, need privacy at all while we're here, I can . . ."

He laughed, sounding cold. "I can take of what I need in the shower if I get too desperate—or maybe you can give me another go."

My expression must have been as stunned as I felt because he added, "Welcome to being roommates, sweetheart."

"I just meant that . . . I don't know. I just didn't want you to think you had to change because you got caught up in my mess," I said, hoping my face wasn't as red as I feared it was.

"I'm not," he said evenly.

"It's not a big town, but maybe there's a girl who—"

"I stopped bringing girls to my bed almost four months ago."

"Four months?" I echoed.

"I thought I met someone I could be with for real." He gave me a sad smile. "It didn't work out like I wanted. Turned out I was just an itch to scratch."

Was he serious? Or was this more of the things he said at Sinners Ink? Was he trying to flirt to make me feel better? I wanted that to be the case almost as much as I wanted it not to be. I looked away. There was nothing else I could do.

"Let me lock up the truck," he said quietly, drawing me out of my musing. "Then we'll get settled in for the night . . . or we can go out to eat, if you want."

"I want to stay here."

He nodded and went back outside.

I didn't want to want him like I did, but I couldn't shove it all away as easily in this tiny house. We were trapped together for at least a few weeks. If I could convince him to leave me here, I could hide out for a while. He could go home. Everything would be okay. He'd be safe from me, and I'd figure the rest out after that.

ADAM

Adam debated what to tell Sasha. She seemed to clinging to the illusion that Tommy was going to change. Part of him wanted to let her, but the rest of him thought about the call Tommy had made the day before he died. Adam hadn't told Sasha about that.

Tommy had let Adam know that he had scored four kilos of coke, and that he would be busy all day so he asked him to "check in on Sugar." Now that he knew from Sasha that she had given Tommy *two* kilos, Adam knew that meant Tommy had cut the coke and then tried to pass it off as worth more than it was. Even with a solid forty-thousand-dollar deal, Tommy had to get greedy. *That* was likely what got him killed. Instead of keeping it simple, he had to try to get just a little more out of what was already a risky deal.

While he was out checking about work, Adam had stopped by the Joshua Tree library. It was a tiny place, but he was able to get online and see if there was any news in the digital edition of the *Verde View*. The only other option was Coyote Corner—which had free wi-fi, showers for hikers, climbing gear and sundries for sale. Adam didn't have a laptop though, so the library was his only recourse.

It didn't take long to find and print the article. Seeing Tommy's name in the news wasn't new. He'd been arrested a few times, usually it was nothing he couldn't plead down or squirm out of. This time, there was no pleading out: He was dead and would soon to be in the ground. Seeing the article made that truth seem worse.

The Rio Verde Police Department released the identity of a body found on Tuesday behind the Fry's Grocery on Ocotillo Street.

The body of Thomas 'Tommy' Holloway, a 25-year-old resident of Rio Verde, was discovered at about 1:30 a.m.

"It appears Holloway had been shot to death," Officer Michaels said. The Rio Verde Police Department has declined further comment.

The unemployed Holloway had a record for misdemeanor drug possession, drunk and disorderly, and resisting arrest

Anyone with information about the case is asked to contact the Rio Verde Police Department Homicide Unit.

Adam wasn't ready or able to speculate much. It didn't really matter. He and Sasha had left Rio Verde. If they needed to move on from Joshua Tree, they would. There were literally hundreds of tiny towns where they could hole up under the radar until the mess in Rio Verde shook itself out. There was no reason for either of them to head back there ever, and unless someone caught wind of where they were now, they would be safe.

The problem was that Adam wasn't sure how motivated anyone would be to look for Sasha. She had what she called "a lot" of cash, and she'd taken it from a man who was now dead. There were others there, though. What was to say that she'd be the target? On the other hand, she also stole a bunch of coke. That was easier to trace, and since her ex was the one who had it, that put her in the crosshairs. Adam's instinct was that they ought to stay out of touch with anyone in Rio Verde, and if necessary, they'd move on. Maybe he was overreacting, though. He needed more information before he could decide just how likely it was that anyone would come looking. How much money was "a lot"?

He stopped in one of the only tattoo shops in town, Mezcal Johnny's—which was actually owned by a veteran artist called Drunk Dave—and told Dave that he wanted to work off the books for a couple weeks. The weathered old artist, who hadn't ever had a single drink in all the times Adam had walked into a bar or cafe with him, simply nodded and asked, "You need a place to bunk?"

"Already handled."

Dave nodded his head and turned away. His black and gray braid was decorated by tiny bright blue feathers that made Adam's eyes widen. "That's new. The feathers . . ."

"One of granddaughters is staying with us for a while," Dave explained. "The wife thinks I should let her treat me like a doll of some sort, so I have feathers and beads and glitter in my hair some days." He shrugged. "What can you do?"

Adam grinned. Dave was unabashedly dedicated to his family. He lived out here along the edge of the park, still climbed and went bouldering despite his advanced age, and was securely under the thumb of his wife. His kowtowing to her was enough that a lesser man would've been embarrassed. Dave was still sporting the kind of muscles that made quite clear that he was anything but weak.

"Day after tomorrow good for you? I can take the girls over to that shopping place they like." Dave looked at the book. "I have a regular here tomorrow."

Shrugging, Adam said, "Whatever shifts you have to spare."

Regular clients were the better paying, more interesting jobs. They were the ones who got a bigger piece of work, like a full back or a sleeve or in some cases even a body suit. They were the Michelangelo jobs, the ones that made an artist memorable. The walk-ins were the daily wage work. It was sometimes still satisfying, but not like the big pieces. Those were the kind of thing that made an artist stay a little longer in a town.

Schedule sorted for now, Adam turned to go, but before he had gone a few steps. "I'm guessing you might leave as suddenly as you arrived, so let's play it by day."

Adam looked back at him and nodded. "Probably good idea."

"Nothing around this time of year but the tail end of tourists and locals who don't get into other people's business," Dave added. "If I hear anything you might want to know, I'll tell you."

"Anyone asking questions about anyone from Rio Verde," Adam told him. "My cousin got himself shot a few days ago."

Drunk Dave bobbed his head once. "Sorry about your cousin. He the one who was all mixed up in the junk?"

"That's Tommy. What got him killed, I suspect."

"Nasty business." Dave might have said more, but the shop phone rang and he turned away then to answer it. "Mezcal's. Dave speaking."

He lifted his hand in a farewell gesture, and Adam left the shop.

WHEN HE GOT BACK to the house, Sasha was pacing. She didn't look as bad as he'd seen her when she'd first got clean, but there was an edge to her that he recognized far too well.

"Are you holding?" he asked.

She stopped and leveled a glare at him. "If I was, I'd have used it already." With visible effort, she took several calming breaths and then added, "Sorry. I'm a little tense."

He quirked a brow at her.

She rubbed her hands up her arms like she was cold. "I'm not using, Adam. I'm just edgy over everything, and it kind of hit me when you were out."

There weren't any words that would make what she was feeling any less awful, so he didn't bother trying to find them. She looked so lost, her bright green eyes dull with worry that he ignored all of the warning signs he'd put up as he closed the distance between them and pulled her into his arms, quietly inhaling the scent of soap and flowers that he always loved. He hugged her and held her tightly. That was the best answer he could offer. Stroking her reassuringly wasn't very helpful when she was acting like she was craving drugs. He sure as hell wasn't going to go score anything for her. That left physical distraction . . . and he didn't think it was a good idea to offer to help her forget by warming the sheets with him. That had complicated things.

He wanted more, but she had walked away. Maybe friendship was all they could have.

"I was worried," she admitted. "What if they came? What if you were hurt? What if—"

"We're fine," he reminded her.

After a few minutes, she stepped away.

He hated how empty his arms felt without her in them. He wished she was in his arms because she wanted him, but he'd given her enough clues, practically come out and said that he loved her and she still wasn't going for it. Even after spending an amazing night together, she was rejecting him.

"Thank you," she murmured. Then she went to the sofa and sat with her legs curled under her. "I unpacked and organized the cupboards. I figure we'll need to find the grocery, but I couldn't go on my own so—"

"How much money?"

"What?"

"How much cash did the corpse have?" he clarified. He sat next to her, but he resisted the urge to touch her.

"A trunk full," she said. "We each got about two hundred and ten thousand dollars, and then there was the coke."

"How many people?"

"Six."

Adam did the math and stared at her for a moment before saying, "Almost one and half million dollars."

She nodded.

The fear of what that could mean for her was enough to make him want to push her faster than he was sure she was able to handle. Adam sat on the sofa and stared at her for a moment.

"I told you I was trouble to be around," she whispered.

"You should've left town the night it happened," he said as levelly as he was able.

Then a horrible thought hit him. "Did they *all* walk away with two kilos and the cash?"

Mutely, she shook her head.

"How many?"

"Just me," she admitted. Her face flushed in guilt as she added, "I couldn't walk away from it. They had no idea how much money it was worth, and I don't think most of them had any connections to sell it, and . . ."

"And you're an addict who was faced with a huge temptation," Adam finished when her words faded. "Seeing that much coke in one place had to have been hard."

"That's why I took it to Tommy right away," Sasha said.

He knew her, knew that she wasn't using again. He'd seen her and Tommy both enough when they were high to know exactly what she was like when she was using. That was the glue that kept her with his cousin: drugs and the way Tommy used them to lure her back when she got free of him.

He pulled out the article and handed it to her, stopping any chance of hearing the admissions that would be a knife to his gut. "Here."

She read it to herself, stopping after the first few lines to glance at him but otherwise motionless. When she was done, she said, "Do you think they'll find the people who did it?"

Adam had thought about it enough to be able to answer promptly. "No. He wasn't important enough, and with his record, they'll assume it was because of a drug deal gone bad. No one cares about criminals killing criminals unless it spills over to the rest of the town."

It wasn't a pretty answer, but in the real world, police were overworked, understaffed, underpaid, and if some punk with a gun was going to eliminate another bad seed, it wasn't necessarily a priority investigation. First came crimes against the taxpayers who supported the police or any co-ed whose injury or absence would make national news *or* hurt enrollment at ASURV. The university brought jobs and revenue. Crimes against small-time dealers weren't a priority.

"So do you think the police will do anything about the other guy? The one who died at the Cave?" Sasha asked.

Adam shook his head. "The only way that would happen is if someone there talked or the body turned up where there'd be bad press if they were ignoring it."

"The body won't turn up."

"You can't be sure of—"

"It was cremated," she interrupted.

For a moment, Adam was speechless. "No body. No money. No drugs. What about the car?"

"Gone."

"So unless that gets unearthed and somehow tracked back to the shop, no one at the P.D. should come looking for you. They're not the problem." He glanced toward the darkening desert sky outside the house. "But almost one and a half million dollars and two kilos of cocaine? Someone's going to be looking for that."

He pulled Sasha close so she was nestled against his side. Adam tried to ignore the warmth that radiated from her body and did very inappropriate things to his imagination.

"We wait it out, Sash. I can keep you hidden for as long as we need," he promised her. "We start over. A new life away from there, and we watch the papers to see if anything happens to any of the others."

"I don't know all of their names."

"So we write down what you do know so we don't forget. It could be months or years or never until this is all resolved." Adam stroked her back, trying to help relax her.

"It seems like there should be something else we can do," she murmured. "Tommy *died* because of this."

That was it, the opening he couldn't resist. Gently, he told her, "No. He died because he cut the coke and tried to sell four kilos. He got greedy and tried to add a con. He died because he was . . . who he was."

She stared at him with tears shining in her eyes as he told her what he knew, and when he was finished, she said, "He wasn't ever going to stop, was he?"

Adam shook his head. "He wasn't a bad guy, but he wasn't ever going to be the one to give you that little house with flowers in front and road trips to Coachella or the music festival at Telluride." He stroked her cheek and added, "You can still have those things, though."

He didn't add that he wanted to be the one to give them to her, but he hoped she would figure that out when she was ready.

SUGAR

I jotted down what I could remember from the night of the shooting.

Adam read it, suggested I hide it, and then we went about living together in our rental house, hoping that trouble didn't follow us along the highway to this little outpost in the desert. It wasn't a perfect plan, but short of turning everything over to the cops and hoping they could keep us safe, there wasn't a better option. And, truthfully, I don't think either of us was the sort to have a lot of faith in the police.

I didn't know whose drugs and cash we had, didn't know the name of the dead guy, and didn't know who killed Tommy—or if it was tied to the murder or Tommy's trying to con whoever he was selling the coke to. I thought about the things that had happened, but it left me worried and stressed so I tried to forget Rio Verde and everything about it.

Except Adam. He was unforgettable and at my side constantly.

Despite everything, the first few days living together went well. I was relieved that I hadn't had to leave him behind, but I wasn't sure how long I could live with him without my feelings for him boiling over into something I couldn't handle right now.

At least, he wasn't calling me out on the night we'd shared. I was wrong to let him thing I had used him, but I was terrified to let him stay. What if they came after me? What if they hurt him? But by the end of the second week, I was starting to feel trapped —or maybe I just had too much time to think about everything that could go wrong.

Adam had to leave. I could look after myself. It was my mess.

But every time I broached the subject, he shook his head and went to work out again—as if that would help my resolve.

I wrote up my notes from the shop, and Adam and I picked up two burn phones so we could reach one another if necessary. Aside from a few short hours when he worked, there wasn't much chance of needing them. We were together most of the time. There wasn't a lot of tattoo work in Joshua Tree, and I hadn't looked for a job yet. I'd gone out to the grocery store once. I'd gone for a few walks, and I'd read almost the entire stack of novels that were at the house.

"I can't do this," I announced as I walked into the main room to find Adam working out *again*. Seeing him doing crunches and push-ups every day wasn't doing much for my resolve to convince him to go. There was just something sexy about a man exercising . . . or maybe it was sexier because it was *Adam* exercising. He was already on the verge of being more defined than most sculptures in a museum. He was just as untouchable, too.

When he stopped at whatever ridiculous number he was at, he sat and looked up at me. "Can't do what?"

"This," I said. Words were too hard suddenly. Maybe I needed to pretend that it was just like with sculptures: There were security guards and alarms that would sound if I gave in to the urge to trail my fingertips over the sharp lines of his body. Smothering the moan that threatened to spill out, I shoved my traitorous thoughts away and made a point not to look at him as he finished his set of push-ups.

"This . . . what? Can you be a little more specific here, Sash?"

I flopped down on the sofa. He'd folded the bed up every day so the room wasn't any smaller than it already was. Still, my body tightened at the thought that I was on what was essentially his bed.

"Sasha?"

My gaze dropped to him. Sweat trickled down his throat and disappeared under his shirt. I stared like I'd never seen him working out. I had. I'd seen it far too often lately. I swallowed and forced my gaze upward.

That wasn't any better.

He was watching me intently, and I knew I couldn't even try to pretend I wasn't ogling him. "Oh, come on, Adam! You know you're eye candy. What am I to do? Pretend you don't look like" —I gestured vaguely at him—"*that?*"

He grinned. "I didn't say a word."

"It doesn't mean anything that I look," I muttered. "Anyone with eyes would look."

His lips twitched, but he didn't say anything. He stood, pulled his shirt off and walked to the door to the bathroom. It felt like a challenge or an invitation, but I couldn't accept either one. My resolve was just weakened by being in the tiny house with him all of the time.

Adam was off limits. I'd slipped once, but twice? Twice would be different. Twice would mean he might stay—or that my heart would break when he didn't.

He was forbidden . . . which meant that all I could do was look.

And damn, was I looking!

He was hot, muscled, tattooed, and wearing only a pair of shorts.

"Sasha?"

I was suddenly sure that it might be cooler outside in the mid-morning desert sun than it was in the house. It was criminal that he looked that good, and I couldn't do anything about it.

"Nope." I looked away. I was starting to think the alternative was to surrender any and all common sense. *Friends. Friends. Friends.* I chanted the word in my head. It was what I needed to remember. We might be hiding away in the desert, but we were friends. I knew it was a bad idea to cross that line when we weren't in a small house together, and I had to be able to remember it was a bad idea here. I listed all of the facts in my head: He was my friend; he was Tommy's cousin; he wasn't going to stay with me forever; there were a lot of girls he'd been with, but none of them lasted for more than a few days; he deserved better.

The facts did nothing to ease the need to touch him.

"Sash?"

I looked over my shoulder to where he stood in the doorway.

"I like that you look." His eyes swept me from top to bottom slowly. "I look at you, too. I have for a long time. I'd like to repeat the n--"

"No!" I swallowed. I wasn't going to think about that night because . . .

"I think about it. You. Us." His voice was gentle, but huskier.

ALL OF MY reasons suddenly seemed hard to remember. With effort, I looked at him and said, "Get your shower. I want to get out of the house."

He stared a moment longer and then turned away.

My heart felt like it was beating faster than it should, and I thought about him naked under the water. I wondered, not for the first time, if he touched himself when he was in there.

I wondered what he thought about if he did.

Guiltily, I hoped it was me.

WHEN ADAM WALKED out of the bathroom, he looked like an invitation to all the sins I wanted to commit. He had a towel slung around his hips. Water droplets slid over his abs and vanished under the towel.

"Put on your fucking pants."

"You're in my bedroom," he reminded me. With no further warning, he dropped the towel.

"Christ, Adam!" I snapped, turning my back to him—but not before I caught a glimpse of his cock, which even at rest was a beautiful sight.

"If it makes you feel better, you can walk into my bedroom naked too." His voice was the only sound in the room, and the silence made it more difficult to erase the brief glimpse of him, the memories of him already seared into my mind.

Naked. Beautiful. Tattooed.

My eyes were closed as if that would make the images vanish.

The zipper of his pants was far too loud for my already screaming lust. I wanted that to be the sound of him unzipping, of the start of something, but I needed him to have the willpower I couldn't find.

"I'm ready," Adam said.

It could've been my ridiculous level of need, but I felt like he was saying he was ready for a lot more than heading into town. I turned and took in the jeans he'd pulled on. "It's too hot for jeans."

"No shorts on the Harley, doll." He shook his head. "As much as I like seeing your legs, you need them covered unless you want to take the truck."

"Jeans. I have jeans," I said hurriedly. I wanted the closeness of being on the bike, straddling him . . . my mind blanked on words at the thought of straddling him.

Sex on the bike.

"Boots too, babe," he said as I darted into the bedroom.

In a matter of minutes, I'd rifled through my drawers, found a pair of skinny jeans, tugged on a pair of tall black leather boots, and grabbed my purse. When I walked into the main room, Adam had laced up his heavy boots and had a leather vest over his shirt.

He surveyed me and announced, "If you're going to ride with me regularly, we need to get you a little more protection than t-shirts and clubbing boots."

"Says the man who refuses to wear a helmet."

"My bike, my rules." He motioned toward the door.

After I stepped outside, the desert heat seemed intense enough that I almost reconsidered the bike. The Explorer had air conditioning. That sounded pretty good right now.

Then Adam climbed on the Harley, and a moment later, I heard the engine growl. He looked back at me, raised his brows questioningly, and any thought of air conditioning vanished.

But I couldn't move. Adam was sitting in front of me, waiting for me, in front of the house we were sharing in the desert. There were some pretty serious threats back in Rio Verde, and the man I'd been dating on and off for two years was dead. I didn't deserve to feel any happiness.

I felt guilt wash over me because I *did* feel a moment of happiness. I wanted Adam, and he was here with me like a bodyguard, friend, and caretaker all in one. I was safe with him at my side. I hadn't ever wanted anything to happen to Tommy, but I couldn't give up on happiness because it had. Two weeks had passed, and although I still felt horrible for what happened, I was starting to admit to myself that while Tommy had loved me, I hadn't loved him.

Not that I loved Adam either.

We were friends, and I cared about him, and heaven help me, I wanted him more than I could handle lately.

"Climb on, Sash," he ordered.

I swallowed my guilt and nerves, walked over, and straddled the bike. I wrapped my arms tightly around him and leaned close. I raised my voice a little, "Adam?"

He glanced back and met my eyes.

"I want you," I admitted. "I'm trying not to, but that night?"

For a moment, he stared at me, our gazes locked.

"I knew I was leaving, and it gave me the excuse." I licked my lips. I could blame it on the dry desert air, but I suspect we both knew that wasn't why my mouth was parched. "I don't have any other excuses."

Then he said, "Hold tight."

And we were off. The needle tipped far enough that I felt a thrill at the speed we were traveling. Out here, beyond stoplights and pedestrians, there was a freedom that I needed. Maybe it was what I'd always needed—a thrill that wasn't deadly.

"More," I yelled.

He laughed, but he increased the speed again. I wouldn't trust just anyone like this, but Adam would keep me safe. He handled the motorcycle like he'd been born to it.

Once he slowed down, I leaned my face on his shoulder.

I kept one arm tightly around him, but I let my right hand drop lower so it rested between his legs. He swerved slightly for a moment, and I knew what I was doing was dangerous in so many ways. I stroked him through his jeans. Slowly.

He slowed the bike down further until we were well under speed now. Any slower and we might as well park. I was pretty sure that I could run as fast as we were rolling, but I didn't need speed now that I had him under my hand. The Harley's engine purred like it was several-hundred-pound vibrator underneath us. Adam controlled it, had the power, and I felt like in that moment, I had the power over him.

I popped the button on his jeans and started to work the zipper down.

"Sasha," he growled.

But I couldn't speak. I just pressed my chest closer to his back and slid my hand inside his jeans as far as I could without his cooperation.

He didn't say another word, just steered the bike to the side of the road and stopped. He supported the bike with one foot on the ground, but he didn't kill the engine.

"Tell me what's going on here." He started to turn back to look at me, but I couldn't handle that.

With my free hand, I quickly stopped him with a steadying touch to his cheek. "Shhh."

For several moments, he stayed like that, perfectly still with my hand in his jeans. His breathing grew harsh enough that I could hear the need in him mixed with the sounds of the still running machine beneath us. It was strangely perfect: the bike still but running, the straining muscles of Adam's body motionless but for involuntary surges of his cock in my hand. I closed my eyes and gave myself over to the sensations of restrained power all around me.

My panties were wet enough that I was starting to think I'd soak through my jeans too. I moaned as Adam thrust against my hand.

"You're going to be the death of me," he muttered.

He killed the engine and dropped the kickstand.

And just like that, I froze.

He started to turn to look at me, but I kept my left hand on his cheek. My right hand was motionless, but my fingers were still wrapped as much as they could be around the width of the delectable cock I'd been dreamed of since the night we shared.

"What do you want here?" he asked in a strained voice.

"To feel you," I whispered.

"You are."

"Do you want me to stop?"

He let out a sound somewhere between a laugh and a groan. "No."

A moment passed, a heartbeat to treasure my power over him.

Then he asked, "Can I touch you?"

"No," I whispered, already resuming stroking him.

"Damn, Sash . . ." he started. Then I felt him swallow before he continued, "I don't want a mess on my bike or my jeans either. Can we—"

"Just this. No sex." I wasn't sure why that mattered, but right now, this was all I wanted. It was all I could be okay with. Touching Adam, pleasing him, that felt good to me. "I don't want you to touch me."

This time there was silence.

After a few more moments, I said, "Close your eyes." Then I slid from behind him. "Turn so you're not straddling the bike."

"Can I open my eyes to do that?"

I smiled. "Yes, but then close them and lean against the bike."

He did as I ordered, and I moved so I was in front of him. Carefully, I eased his jeans down a little and freed him. "Keep your eyes closed, Adam."

He moaned as I leaned forward and took him in my mouth. He was big enough that I had to relax my throat to work past the gag reflex, but he was patient. He didn't thrust forward or do anything to make me regret my choices. His hands were at his sides, curled into tight fists as if he was holding some invisible leash of self-control.

I swallowed around him, taking him further into my throat than I'd ever managed without panic before now.

Adam moaned.

I reached out and took one of his hands and led him to my hair. I wanted him to hold on to me.

He tangled his fingers in my hair as I released his hand.

I lifted my other hand to cup his balls.

"Fuck," he moaned. "You're perfect."

I sped up, lacing my fingers with his where he was touching my head and caressing his balls with my other hand, until he came in my mouth with a growl.

"More than perfect," he said in a rough voice. "You're a fucking goddess, Sasha."

I pulled away, leaning back on my heels. The man I'd fantasized about every night in my bed since leaving Rio Verde—and a lot of nights before that--was staring down at me like I was everything he wanted too. For a moment, I wanted to ignore reality and treasure the look on his face.

He yanked me to my feet and slanted his mouth across mine to kiss me like every word he'd said when I was on my knees was gospel truth. I know smart girls knew not to believe the things people said in the moment, but as he kissed me like it was a promise, I came damn close to believing him.

When he paused, he whispered, "Can I touch you?"

Mutely, I shook my head and closed my eyes.

He rested his forehead against mine and murmured, "I won't hurt you, Sash. Did I do something before that's made you run?"

"No." I shook my head again. I wanted him. I couldn't even pretend otherwise any more. That didn't mean I could be what he needed. I was too messed up, and sooner or later, he'd notice. Right now, we were alone together, so he didn't have a lot of options. Later, when he realized and left me, it would destroy me. I shouldn't have even touched him, but I'd been dreaming of him for so long that I was weak.

"I can't. I just . . . can't," I whispered.

He was silent, but he pulled me into a tight hug and said, "We'll see."

Then he set himself to rights, and we climbed back on the Harley like I hadn't just given him head alongside the road in the middle of the day.

SUGAR

Joshua Tree was a tiny speck of a town, perfect for being unfound for a while, but that also meant that it wasn't a place where jobs were going to be easy to find. There were a few little stores, thrift shops, climbing supplies, and a pizza place. All told, I'd guess that the permanent residents of the town numbered under ten thousand people. My chances of many job options weren't good.

I didn't really need the money, but I was going to go crazy without something to fill my days.

Adam stopped the bike in front of a restaurant called The Crossroads Cafe. I slid off the back of the Harley.

He turned to face me, but I wasn't able to look him in the eye. He stayed on the bike, but he grabbed my hand and kept me from walking away.

"Are we okay?" he asked.

"I think so."

"Did you think I expected—"

"No!" I felt my face burn in mortification. "That was my choice, Adam. I know you don't . . . I mean, I don't know what I mean."

He hugged me, somewhat awkwardly because he was still on the Harley.

"I didn't, um, take advantage of you, did I?" I mumbled the words against his shoulder.

He pushed me away and looked into my eyes. "Not at all." Then his voice turned teasing and he added. "I'm not *that* easy, Sash. I don't do anything with my body that I don't want to, okay?"

I nodded and quickly turned away.

Behind me, he said, "I wanted you before, too. You didn't use me. You're my . . . closest friend."

My heart sunk at his words. *Friends.* That's what we really were, friends. He'd enjoyed being with me. I had no doubts there. It didn't mean anything, though, not to him.

"I want to take care of you," he added.

I glanced back. "I can handle myself."

This time Adam grinned and said, "Mmmm. Can I at least watch?"

I knew better, knew I was playing with the kind of fire that would burn a hole in my heart, but the words just slipped out: "Maybe later."

He took a deep breath, grabbed me, and kissed me until I was ready to promise a lot more. My heart might not recover, but more southern parts of me weren't concerned with my future broken heart.

Mutely, I jerked open the door to the restaurant, the Crossroads Café. It was mostly charming. I liked the weathered tables and the wooden . . . everything. The walls, the bare rafter ceiling, the bar, it was all wood. I loved that part. The people inside where varied and interesting. A man with long grey dreadlocks sat chatting with a girl in a retro 1950s cherry-covered dress. Climbers and hikers, dust covered and sun hardened, lined the bar.

The waitress led us to a table, and I continued to think the little cafe was pretty fabulous—up until I saw the dead cat on the wall. I didn't know my wildlife well enough to say what it was. It was bigger than a housecat, smaller than a mountain lion. I think it was a bobcat, although I wouldn't swear to that. Whatever it was called, it was dead and standing on a ledge. I shuddered and turned away from it, quickly taking the chair that put my back to the taxidermied animal.

"Are you cold?" Adam asked as the waitress left to grab menus.

I lowered my voice and told Adam, "I don't like dead things." I gestured behind me. "I remember going to a natural history museum in high school. I had nightmares for weeks afterward. Seeing animals with glass eyes and slowly fading, decaying pelts seems like the stuff of horror movies."

"So . . . *Night at the Museum?*"

"Right there with most horror movies in my book," I answered.

The waitress returned, putting our conversation on hold, and we ordered drinks.

"Dave says they're hiring," Adam mentioned when the waitress walked away again. "They had a waitress quit yesterday with no notice. You could apply, assuming you can handle the dead cat watching your every move . . . "

I laughed in spite of myself. "If I have taxidermy dreams . . . "

"You can wake me, and I'll hold you," Adam finished.

Whatever I would've said next vanished. I wasn't even sure if I'd had a thought that I'd just forgotten or if my brain had totally fritzed. The tension flared to life between us again, but for me, this wasn't just about lust. Adam would take care of me; he had been in little ways for months when we were in Rio Verde—and he'd been trying well before that. He understood me. He made me laugh. And I thought he was damn near perfect. If I didn't find a way to resist the tension between us, my heart was going to be confetti when he finally left.

The waitress returned with our drinks, took our orders, and left. Adam and I kept staring at one another with so many things unsaid between us. He was my friend, my *best* friend. Mila had been the girl I was closest to, and most of the other girls I knew were the ones I had partied with the past couple of years. Cocaine and booze didn't exactly engender lifelong bonds of trust and mutual respect. It sure as hell didn't make me appealing to any friends I had before Tommy. They'd all drifted away or been pushed away as I grew closer to Tommy and more caught up in his world. Now Tommy was dead, and Mila might as well be dead to me. I couldn't talk to her or see her without endangering us both.

"Sasha?" He sounded worried.

"You're my best friend," I said. "I don't know why you put up with me, but I'm grateful. I don't know if you knew that, but you should. When I was trying to get clean and when I had the flu and now . . . you're a good man, Adam."

He shook his head. "I don't 'put up with you.' There's no one I'd rather be around."

I sipped my drink, both to buy a moment and because my mouth was dry, before saying, "I feel the same. I'd be lost without your friendship. When you leave--"

"I'm not going anywhere without you," he replied tersely.

Adam didn't say anything else, but he seemed tense.

We finished our meal, and I asked to see the manager while Adam walked outside. It didn't take much to get a shot at the job. Apparently, there weren't dozens of people moving into Joshua Tree at the end of May. It wasn't an actual hire, but they were willing to have me come in for a shift or two and see if I worked out.

That plan fit my needs perfectly. It meant no paperwork right now, and *that* was exactly what I needed. If we decided to stay in Joshua Tree, we'd figure out how much of a paper trail we wanted to leave, but as a temp, I could stall on that dilemma.

After that was sorted out, Adam and I meandered through the town, checking out a fun looking pizza shop, an outdoor supply shop, and picked up a few brochures. His theory was that if we were in the area for a few weeks we ought to enjoy it. That was apparently how he traveled: settle in for a little while, check out what the area had to offer, and then move on.

"Why didn't you leave Rio Verde then?" I asked after he explained how he'd lived before coming to check on Tommy.

Adam shook his head. "I was needed there." He stared at me, like he was daring me to ask the question on the tip of my tongue. When I didn't, he said, "Let's head back to the house."

The drive back was uneventful. I kept my fingers laced together, arms around his waist, and did my damnedest not to press my body too tightly to him. I wasn't sure what we were doing, but after talking, I realized exactly how devastated I'd be if I messed up our friendship and lost Adam over a bit of sex. The risk wasn't worth it, even though I knew being in his arms was brain-melting.

When we got to the house, I all but leaped off the bike and hurried inside.

Adam must've decided to give me a moment because he took his time outside, checking something or other on the Harley. It was a much-needed reprieve. Riding with him was harder than ever after our interlude along the road.

My reprieve ended when he walked through the door.

"Let me finish your tattoo."

I didn't know what to say. He was like the serpent in the garden, knowing exactly what to offer to break the resolve I'd been steadily building up. I wanted to say yes, but instead I said, "I can't."

"I'm here; you're here. Why not?" Adam watched me like he expected me to run.

He wasn't wrong to expect it either. I wanted to run. I just wasn't sure whether I wanted to run to or from him. It was probably a bit of both.

"That's a bad idea," I said.

"Because . . . ?"

What was I to say? Because I'm running out of reserves of self-control? That touching him made it worse rather than taking the edge off? Because I wanted him so badly I woke up from dreams that made me moan in my sleep? There was no way I could admit that without doing the very thing that I was trying to avoid—damaging our friendship.

"Let me tattoo you," he urged. His beautiful blue eyes widened, and he added, "Please?"

And I had no other answer I could give him. "Sure," I whispered. "But be . . . like you would with a stranger, not like you . . . not those things you said before."

His mouth curved in a dangerous smile before he asked, "So I shouldn't use the vibrations of the machine to try to make you come? I could, Sasha. You can trust me."

I nodded, agreeing to all of it—the fact that I was saying he shouldn't, the fact that I wanted him to, and the fact that I trusted him.

"Let me get set up." He turned away, suddenly the professional I'd asked him to be.

I wasn't sure what to do, other than wait. I paced to the tiny kitchen and got a drink of water. I tried not to watch him as he pulled out the case that held his traveling kit. He used it for conventions, but when Tommy and I had visited him at a show in Phoenix, he'd had a temporary set-up that looked a lot like it would in a shop. There was a table, a chair for him, and of course, a counter where all of his supplies were.

"Your bed or mine?"

"The sofa," I said in a surprisingly steady voice, pointing at the sofa which was his makeshift bed.

I watched him as he set out the things he needed to add art to my chest. It wasn't the same as at the shop or at the convention. This was his bed, and we were alone. He was acting like a professional though, setting up supplies and ignoring me like I was no different than any customer.

After a few minutes, he pointed at the sofa. "On the table, Miss Kovac."

I couldn't look at him as I shucked my shirt and dropped my bra. I didn't want to see his eyes when he saw me topless. I'd seen the heat in them the first time I'd peeled my shirt off so he could tattoo my stomach, and it made me crave him so badly that I started to avoid him and made excuses to avoid any work on my tattoo. I'd seen that same obvious lust the night we'd been together. I craved it, wanted him to look at me like he felt as drunk on this as I was.

He didn't look at my face as he carefully swiped my skin with a cleanser or when he began studying the lines of the branches to see where they should extend. Tattooing was more than slapping stock images on some random body part, at least it was when the tattooist was an artist. Adam was an artist.

For several moments, he studied me, his eyes following the lines of my body, and then he nodded to himself. "Ready?"

"Yes," I whispered.

The hum of the machine made my body tighten in excitement, and that first bite of needles on my skin made me gasp. I wasn't a pain junkie, but I knew that the initial pain would fade under the natural chemicals in my body. I had to ride the pain for a few moments, and then a glorious high would follow. That expectation, the joy of getting my art, and the bliss of Adam's hands on my skin combined to make my eyes close. Several minutes passed with only the sound of the tiny motor and the steady breathing of the man wielding it. I didn't mean to, but I moaned a little.

"Are you okay?"

"Very," I admitted.

"Hurt?"

Quietly, I admitted, "No."

He chuckled, a sound that always made my body clench in need lately, and I blushed. "I'm being professional, as requested," he reminded me.

"I know."

"If you change your mind . . ." he offered.

My eyes opened, and I stared up at him. The needles left my skin for a moment as he met my gaze. The heat I'd seen there before was back. I bit my lip to keep from moaning.

"I could make you feel good. Let me, Sasha. Let me make you happy."

I wanted to. God, I wanted to fall apart while he stared down at me. My body was screaming *yesyesyes*, but I shook my head. "Tattoo me, Adam."

Later, I'd think of him like this, his eyes filled with lust as he left his mark on my body in a way no one else ever would. I thought of his admission that he'd only ever been unprofessional with me, that I was the only one he'd only wanted to make orgasm while he etched art into my flesh, and I knew that I could never let anyone else tattoo me. In this, if nothing else, I was always going to be only his.

SUGAR

The next week was somewhere between ludicrous and embarrassing. I volunteered for every shift I could at The Crossroads Cafe, and Adam drove me to and from work in the Explorer. We never once mentioned that Thing That Happened Along The Road, but we didn't take the Harley if we were together. We both acted like I hadn't wanted him desperately, and he hadn't let me touch him and taste him. We didn't acknowledge the way he'd looked at me as he tattooed me. We didn't mention that I was sure we'd both heard the other one moaning through the thin walls in the tiny house late at night.

Our shared silent agreement to try to behave like everything was normal made me feel like I was walking around waiting for something to snap.

Then it did.

I was folding the laundry he'd carried into the house. I wasn't sure if we were staying in the little town or moving on. We hadn't discussed it. All of my fears about drug dealers, police, and killers seemed to have been left in Rio Verde. I should tell him he could leave, but . . . I wanted him to stay. As the days passed, I felt more and more settled. The money from that night at The Coffee Cave sat untouched in the bedroom. I could buy a car with some of it, but that felt like asking Adam to leave . . . which wasn't what I wanted at all.

"Let's go for a ride," he suggested.

I looked up from the t-shirt in my hands. "No."

He walked closer, and I felt like he was stalking me. I didn't want to run though, at least not run *from* him. I shook my head. "It's a bad idea."

"Why?"

I dropped the shirt on the sofa next to me and flopped down on it. "Because we're roommates. Because we . . . I . . . because of last week."

"Did something happen?" He lifted his gaze, and I was pinned by those bright blue eyes.

"Adam . . ."

He shook his head. "I thought something did, but then you've spent the past week all but running if I got within six feet of you. So I figure I must've imagined you looking up at me from my bed like a goddess while I tattooed you. I must've imagined earlier that day when your perfect mouth was—"

"Stop," I begged.

His words stopped, but he walked over to the little table in front of the sofa and shoved it aside with his boot-clad foot. Then he dropped to his knees in front of me. It reminded me painfully of when he tattooed me right here.

I closed my eyes. There was no other option. I couldn't say no if I saw how he was looking at me.

And then his fingertips brushed my skin as he eased my tank top up to expose my stomach. I swallowed. This was when I should say no, when I should tell him to stop. I knew it. This was a bad idea. He didn't do commitments, and I couldn't handle being the girl he fucked a few times and left behind. I couldn't handle him staying and getting hurt.

He was my friend and my fantasy. I didn't want to lose him. Not now. Not ever. I had to stop this before we were any more involved.

I just couldn't *say* it yet. . . not when his lips were on my skin. He kissed my stomach, peppering my skin with the barest touches, and leaving me wanting more. It was gentle in a way that was wholly unfamiliar. Not that Tommy had been my first, but there hadn't been anyone in my life who acted like this. I'd had sex that left me boneless and satisfied, but what Adam was doing wasn't sex like I knew it.

"I have rules, Sash." His words were a hot whisper on my stomach. "I've never broken them before, and I won't now."

"Rules?" I echoed.

"Mm-hmm." His tongue flicked against my belly button. "No one has ever left my bed unfulfilled."

"We were on a bike, not in your bed," I murmured.

He chuckled, but his fingers were already unbuttoning my shorts. "You can play word games, but it won't help, sweetheart. You know damn well that my bike is a hell of lot more personal than my bed, *and* you were in my bed when I tattooed you."

Finally, I opened my eyes and looked down at the man I wanted more than I'd ever wanted drugs or freedom or anything else I'd thought I craved. It all paled next to Adam.

He was kneeling in front of me. My shorts were unbuttoned, but he'd made no move to peel them down yet. The question was there, but he left all of the control in my hands. I could re-button my shorts and push him away.

I *should* do that.

He watched me as he slid both hands over my hips and to my bare legs. Slowly, he traced the outside of my legs. His fingertips grazed my skin, touching so carefully that it was more promise than reality. I found myself holding my breath, wanting that touch desperately even while I told myself I couldn't have it.

"You don't need to—"

"I *do*," he insisted. "I *really* do, Sasha."

"I wasn't asking for . . . anything when I did that." I couldn't look away. It would be so much easier to do the right thing if he wasn't touching me like that, wasn't giving me that tempting taste of what I could have if only I gave in.

"When you wrapped that soft hand around me," he said. "Or when you wrapped those beautiful lips around me until I came?"

Remembering the feel of him, the taste of him, wasn't good for my self-control. "Either," I whispered.

"I need to touch you. I've needed to every hour of every day." His hands stroked back up my legs, pushing them further apart. And I let him. "I need to taste you."

He bent so he could kiss my upper thigh.

"It was torture tattooing you last week. You looked like you were moments from coming, just because I was tattooing you." His voice grew rougher as he added, "All week I've been unable to get you out of my mind. Touching me, then naked here in front me. I need to taste you."

I whimpered.

"Tell me I can, Sash," he murmured as he licked a line to the edge of my shorts. He bit me softly.

My mind was saying, *no, no, no. You can't do this.*

"Yes," I whispered.

I felt his lips curve into a smile while his mouth was still against my thigh. Then he pressed a kiss to me over my clothes. It wasn't even my bare skin, but I couldn't help myself. I arched against his face.

"Please," I added.

It sounded like he said "Thank God," but I couldn't be sure because in the next instant he'd wrapped an arm around my back and carefully pushed me backward on the sofa and was kissing me, his hands stroking any exposed skin they could find.

"You said I could go slower next time," he reminded me. "May I?"

I nodded.

His gaze was hot enough to burn as he looked at me not with the eyes of an artist, but with the eyes of a man. He couldn't miss the stunning artwork he had drawn on my skin, but his eyes were focused on my breasts as his fingers traced the edges of my bra through the thin cotton.

Goose bumps pebbled my skin. I'd pushed him to be harder, faster, the first night we shared.

Tonight, *he* was in control.

There was no rush to his actions, nothing but measured patience as he unraveled every last bit of resistance I had. When his hands started to lift my top, it didn't even occur to me to do anything other than raise my arms and let him draw it off of me.

"Say it."

"Yes, Adam. Slower is fine." The words were nothing but a sigh as his mouth trailed along my ribs.

No one had ever touched me like this before, so tenderly, so reverently.

Then the bra was gone, its cups replaced by his hands. I arched my back, my breath coming in short gasps as need grabbed me by the throat. This was a mistake, but that didn't matter to me anymore. Nothing mattered but the feel of Adam's skin against mine, of his lips skimming over me. He trailed kisses down my body, his tongue flicking out to tease me with the promise of what he was going to do next.

I was naked before I knew it, my body aching with desire. Adam took one quick glance at my face, giving me one last chance to come to my senses and tell him to stop. When I didn't, he lowered his mouth to me.

He was patient with me, teasing me to near madness and then backing off, making the pleasure and torment last. Like he could do this all day and he wouldn't mind not coming himself as long as he pleased me. There were no expectations, no demands, no agenda. He left no doubt in my mind that this was all about me, and the intensity of his focus made me feel like the center of the universe.

When I stopped trembling in the wake of my third orgasm, I finally realized how terrible a risk I was running, how danger-ously seductive it was to let Adam do this to me even once. I felt like I had to run. There was no way I'd survive trying to let go of Adam if we kept going down this path. I'd never been someone who had one-night stands. I didn't sleep with friends casually, and I was the worst sort of fool to think that I could let go after the night we shared in Rio Verde. We were sharing a tiny one bedroom so I understood how our long-ignored sexual tension had turned into this. It would continue to do so as long as he wanted me—and then he'd be gone and I'd be destroyed.

"Stop," I said weakly, trying to pull him up to lie with me on the sofa.

He stayed kneeling on the floor, his hand drawing absent patterns on my bare stomach. Even that was too much though. I'd never thought that the slow, gentle caresses could be as satisfying as the sort of sex I'd always had. Adam proved me wrong repeat-edly over the past . . . however long it had been.

"Thank you," I whispered.

He made a sound of satisfaction. "My pleasure . . . one I'm happy to repeat as often as you let me."

My silence as I tried to come up with an answer was obvi-ously more revealing than I wanted it to be because Adam's voice grew tense as he asked, "What?"

"I can't do this." I covered his hand with mine, and then sat up. "We can't."

"What can't we do?" he asked, slowly pronouncing each word in that calm way that told me he was far from calm.

"This."

Talking about not having sex while sitting naked in front of the man who had just made me buck and writhe and beg wasn't something I wanted to do. I reached for my clothes, and without looking at him, quickly shimmied into my shorts and tank top. I didn't bother with a bra. That could wait.

"I don't want to lose your friendship because we . . ." I started.

He was still kneeling on the floor. It didn't make things any easier. He made a 'go on' gesture with his hand.

"This was . . ." I started and stopped. I simply didn't have the words. *The best experience I've ever had? Even better than the first time? Earth-shattering? Heart-breakingly perfect?* I shook my head and settled for a word that didn't reveal how incredible it had been. "Wonderful, but we can't let it happen." I folded my arms over my chest. "I should've said something before. I took advantage of you last week and back home and--"

He laughed, and not in the way that I liked.

"You're lonely, and you're stuck trying to take care of me," I continued as if he hadn't made a sound. "You need to go back to Rio Verde. Find someone there or . . ."

He stood, turned, and walked out of the room. In another few minutes, I heard the roar of the Harley as he sped off into the desert.

SUGAR

Hours passed, and Adam didn't come back. I know it was stupid, but I needed to hear someone's voice from home. I pulled the SIM card out of the depths of my bag where it had been the past few weeks and shoved it back into my phone. It was just one call, and I was scared, upset, and alone. Mila answered on the third ring.

"Are you okay?" she asked.

"I'm safe. You?"

"I'm okay," she said, but there was enough of a pause there that I worried. Mila was one of those people who didn't share her secrets easily. It was part of why our friendship worked. We both held our cards close.

"I'll listen if—"

"I'm good," she interrupted. "Where are—"

"Don't ask," I said quietly. "I can't say, but I'm safe."

We were quiet for a moment, and maybe it was silly, but I liked the feeling of not being alone even if the person I was talking to was miles and hours away. I didn't know if I'd ever see her again, but tonight, I could hear her voice. It made me feel a little calmer.

Then she said, "Did you see it?"

"See what?"

"Ian. Fucking *Ian* who sang for us while we wiped tables in the Cave," she said with excitement in her voice. "He's all over the television!"

My heart filled with lead at her words. "*He* told?" Of all of the people there, he was one of the ones I thought least likely to spill.

"No! He's on that show, American Voice. He's one of the ones everyone's talking about, and Savannah. Do you know her? Waits tables over at that diner Ian loved. She's there too. Everyone's all 'they're a couple.'" Mila laughed in genuine amusement. "He's been mooning over her forever, but he's never touched her . . . not unless he did it in the last couple of weeks. I'm not perfect, but I sure as fuck wouldn't have been spending nights with him if he was with her. He loves her. She's too blind to see it though . . . sort of like you with Adam. How is he?"

I had closed my eyes while Mila talked. She was in a great mood, and I felt like I could pretend she was with me.

"I don't know. Mad? Gone?" I choked back a sob, but not before she heard it.

"Talk to me," she ordered.

So I did. I told her everything. I didn't spare any of the embarrassing or awkward details, not about how my feelings were clouding my judgment or the fact that I practically assaulted him on the back of the bike.

She laughed at that part. "I *told* you bike sex was awesome!"

"Anything with Adam would be awesome," I muttered pitifully.

"So tell *him*, dumb ass." She sighed. "I swear, Sugar, you're worse than a guy sometimes. Ian wants Savannah, but he tries to keep her as a friend. You and Adam watch one another like you're about to combust if you get too close. You can be friends and lovers. Ian and I were both."

"But you didn't love him," I said, not realizing what I'd admitted until I heard her gasp.

"I knew it! I knew you loved him. Seriously, Tell. Him. Now."

"He's gone! I told you that." I closed my eyes again. "Weren't you listening?"

"He'll be back, Sugar. You know he will. He's been waiting for you to see him for as long as I've seen him coming around, worse since you ditched the . . . Oh, crud! I didn't mean . . . I know he's dead and all. Tommy *was* an asshole though, Sugar."

"Yeah, he was sometimes," I admitted.

We talked a few more minutes, and then I hung up so Mila could handle some vague emergency.

I held the phone for a minute. It was already on, so I checked my messages and my texts. There were a couple messages from Mila, three from Jason, and one from Sinners Ink. There were also a few calls from anonymous numbers. I didn't delete any of them.

After a moment, I called and left a message at Sinners. "Hey, this is Sasha . . . Sugar. I got your message. I'm not sure where Adam is. We didn't stay together. He went to some shop where he used to work. That's all I know."

I thought about calling Jason back. He'd left two very terse messages and one that was almost nice. I felt bad that he was without baristas, but I'd feel a lot worse if I got arrested or killed because of the things that happened at The Coffee Cave. It was a downtime in the year anyhow. He'd be fine training new people.

I pulled the card back out of my phone. I didn't think it was that my phone could used to track me, at least not by the sort of people who might be looking for me. It would be different if it was the police, but the news article that Adam had found was all there was. I was fairly sure no one official was really investigating Tommy's death or the man who'd died at The Coffee Cave.

There probably weren't a lot of people filing missing persons reports on dead drug dealers.

After a while, I sat in the front room, alternating between staring out the window and re-reading one of the regency romance novels that had come with the rental house. It was the second time I'd read it, but it still drew me in.

I wouldn't say that I was waiting up for Adam, but I might admit that I was worried that he wouldn't come home. I wouldn't blame him either. I worried that it was too late to tell him how I felt; I worried that Mila was wrong and he didn't feel anything more than lust and friendship. I worried about the messages on my phone. Jason probably wanted to nag me about work, or maybe he saw the article about Tommy. They'd met a few times when Tommy came by to watch me at work. The anonymous calls made me nervous, but like so much else, there wasn't a thing I could do about them.

Worrying kept me awake for another hour or so, but eventually, I gave in to exhaustion and crawled into bed. My burn phone was on the bed next to me just in case Adam called. I wasn't sure what I'd do if he did call. I didn't know my way around here at all, but I had the keys to the Explorer and if I had to go somewhere to get him, I'd figure it out then.

I was asleep before my head hit the pillow.

It felt like a minute later that the sound of the door slamming woke me suddenly. I glanced at the clock. *4:07.* I had only been asleep an hour or so when I heard Adam come in . . . at least I assumed it was him. In the wake of everything that had happened, I had to check.

I walked to the doorway of the bedroom, opened the door, and looked out at him. I didn't know what to say. He stood in the living room, saddlebags in hand, illuminated by the one small lamp he'd turned on.

I clutched the doorframe with one hand like it could keep me steady.

He obviously wasn't in a forgiving mood because the first thing he said was, "You really didn't think you could pretend it never happened, did you?"

I looked at him, not sure there was an answer that wouldn't lead to an argument I wasn't ready to have. I'd given him an out, the words he needed so he could go on with the way he lived and I could keep my heart from shattering when he did.

He pulled a bottle of whiskey out of his saddlebag and clunked it on the kitchen counter. "Go to bed, *Sugar.*"

"Seriously? You were riding drunk?? Are you an idiot?"

"That's a very good question." Adam twisted the top of the bottle, and I heard the crack of the seal breaking. "I didn't think I was an idiot, but after tonight, I think I was wrong."

He lifted the bottle of Jack Daniels like he was toasting me and then took a swig. He walked toward me, the bottle dangling from his hand, but he didn't touch me. He stopped in front of me and stared down at me.

I folded my arms over my chest. "You could've died."

"Would you care?"

"Don't be an asshole, Adam. Of course, I'd care. You're my friend."

"Right," he said, turning his back on me and walking over to the sofa. He flopped down on it and then lifted the bottle again. His gaze never left me as he chugged his whiskey.

"I'm sorry. I wasn't trying to be rude," I said. "You weren't disappointing or anything."

He quirked his brow. "Well, there's that at least. I'd hate to be a lousy fuck . . . oh, wait, we didn't do *that*. It's okay for you to suck my cock or for me to make you come over and over on my tongue, but no more sex. That's the line, right?"

"Don't be crude," I snapped.

"Don't be a . . . shit, Sasha, I don't even know what you're being." He shook his head. "I don't think this is how *friends* act though. I thought we were finally getting somewhere, and you stab me in the heart."

"I did *what?*"

He ignored my question and kept rambling, "I would've ridden drunk too. Drunk Dave tossed my ass in his car and had his crazy wife drive me out while he rode my bike here. Do you know how long it's been since I was angry enough to ride drunk? *Years,* Sasha. It's been years, but . . . " He lifted his hands in an exaggerated gesture of what-can-you-do. "You stabbed me."

"I didn't stab you," I muttered.

"Did."

I sighed and asked, "*Drunk* Dave rode your Harley?"

Adam waved his hand. "He doesn't actually drink. Jus' a name, *Sugar.*"

"So, you went out, got drunk, Drunk Dave brought you home, and now you're sitting here with another bottle of whiskey?" I summarized.

"Got it in one." He patted the sofa. "Come sit with me."

"Why?" I was already walking toward him though. I couldn't refuse him.

"Because I don't care if you're Sugar or Sasha, I want you near me." He took another drink. "I can't change everything, but if what you want is an asshole like Tommy, I can be like that. Hell, I *used* to be like that. Sometimes the things you got to do to take care of your family aren't legal. Shit happens. It wasn't the life I wanted though. It'll kill you. It killed him. But I've tried to be a better person, gave up the only bad habit I had left, and you still went to him instead of me."

I all but fell onto the sofa as he talked. My knees felt weak, and my hands were shaking. I opened my mouth, but no words came.

"Girls feed you all these lines about wanting a good guy, but not you. You want an asshole. Right, *Sugar?*" He lifted the bottle again, but this time I grabbed it before he took a drink.

Carefully, I pried the bottle out of his hand and set it on the floor in front of me. "Stop."

He didn't reach for it. He just stared at me.

"I don't understand," I admitted. "I didn't mean to hurt you or . . ."

Adam shook his head. "You're the only girl I've ever felt like this about. I want to see you all the time, and not just naked . . . Naked was good. Great really."

He looked at me like there was a question there, and I nodded and said, "It was earth-shattering for me."

"Then why did you kick me out?"

"I didn't!"

"You didn't say 'get out' but it was what you meant. 'Go back to Rio Verde, Adam. Go fuck someone else, Adam.'" He shook his head. "I don't want anyone else, Sasha. All I can see is you. All I want is you. I can't be with anyone else. I *tried*. I couldn't fuck her."

"Oh."

He grabbed my hand. "So if you need me to be an asshole, I can. Just give me time to change."

"You're an idiot," I whispered. "I don't want you to change."

Instead of looking relieved, his expression grew cloudier. "So no matter what I do, it's a no?"

"No!"

"No what? No you won't give me a chance? Or no . . . something else?" He frowned.

"No changing. I like *you,* but I thought you were just being nice. I know how you are though. I figured if we *did* have sex again, I couldn't handle it when you leave me later because you don't have relationships."

"You're an idiot, too." He sounded a little awed, so even though the words were harsh, I didn't think they were an insult. He proved that a moment later when he added, "I didn't have anyone permanent in my life because none of them were *you*."

He bent his head to kiss me, but he pulled away after a moment.

"What?"

"I've been wanting you for almost two years and waiting for you to notice for months. I'm not making love to you now that we're on that same page when I'm drunk." He wrapped his arms around me and tugged me on to his lap. "Just let me hold you."

After a few moments, I shook my head and got out of his lap. "I have a better plan."

I grabbed his hand tugged. He stood, steady despite the fact that he was definitely drunk.

"Sleep next to me," I said, leading him to the bedroom.

"I'm keeping my jeans on," he muttered, like I was some great seductress trying to steal his honor. "Maybe my boots."

I laughed. "No boots."

He scowled. "Okay, but I'm just sleeping, nothing else. If I don't need to be an asshole to be with you, we're doing things right from here out."

SUGAR

I was confused when the shrill sound of the phone ringing woke me up. I was even more confused when I realized I was wrapped up with Adam. I'd had this dream before, but when I woke, I was alone. I smiled. He was real, and he was in my bed.

"What the fuck is that noise?" he muttered.

"Phone."

"I'll give you anything you want if you make it stop. Mansions. Jewels. Private islands." He opened his eyes and gave me a pitiful look. "Anything."

I laughed and went to answer the phone while Adam stumbled to the bathroom. I was still smiling when I picked up the phone in the main living area. Adam was in my bed. Adam wanted to be with me for real. It was like someone had just dropped my biggest wish into my lap.

On the other end of the phone, a man asked, "Is this Sasha or Sugar or whatever that drunk bastard said your name was?"

My heart had started racing, waking me better than caffeine would, when someone asked for me. All I could think was that they had found me. Then I realized that it was a call for Adam. My terror ebbed as quickly as it had arrived.

"Maybe."

"Tell Adam to take the day off. Shaky hands have no place in tattoo shops," the man barked.

"Thank you," I said.

As I spoke, Adam walked into the living room bare-foot. He hadn't bothered to put on a shirt like he usually did the past week, and that little detail was enough to make my heart speed up again . . . but for a reason other than fear this time.

The way he stared at me, like there was nothing else in the world, made my mouth dry and my panties wet.

I stared at Adam and said, "I'll tell him you called . . . I'm guessing this is Not Really Drunk Dave."

Dave laughed. "I like that . . . and who's this? That boy called you a couple different names."

"Sasha. My name is Sasha," I said, looking up at the amazing, tattooed, beautiful man who was now stalking across the room toward me. "And as of this morning, I'm pretty sure I'm Adam's girlfriend."

I let out a yip as Adam pulled me against him and took the phone. "Sasha's busy now. I was a fucking idiot last night. I owe you. Hanging up now."

Then he dropped the phone and looked at me. "I'm not drunk anymore."

I slid my hands up his bare chest and wrapped my arms around his neck. He grabbed my ass and lifted me so I was wrapped around him. I pressed my body closer to him. "Let's continue this discussion in the shower . . . and then the bedroom . . . and maybe the kitchen."

He growled and kissed me. The taste of toothpaste was much nicer than the whiskey I'd tasted at four in the morning. He still smelled vaguely like whiskey, but I wasn't complaining. He tasted like heaven, and he felt like everything I'd ever wanted.

There were a lot of words to describe the way I felt when I

was hoisted in the air with my legs around Adam. Amazing. Free. Lucky. *Happy*. They all worked for me.

"Need to shower, and I need you. I have a plan . . ."

"Okay." I would've agreed to anything. A shower with Adam was certainly no hardship.

"It wasn't just drunk dreams, right?"

"I was sober and remember the same thing," I assured him. "You and me. Admitting we have feelings."

"More than *feelings*, Sash." He walked us to the bathroom, carrying me with such ease that it was like I weighed nothing. I wasn't particularly tall or heavy, but Adam moved like I was weightless . . . and I simply enjoyed being in his arms and against his bare chest. I'd enjoy it a lot more if I wasn't wearing a shirt.

"Let me down," I said when he stepped inside the bathroom.

He frowned, but he lowered me so I could put my feet on the floor. "Is everything . . ."

His words faded as I peeled my shirt off and shoved my sleep shorts and panties down. They puddled at my feet, and I stepped out of them. I wasn't ashamed of my body, and if I had been, the way he was looking at me in the bright light of morning as I stripped would've ended any doubts I had. I wasn't built like a model, but it was obvious that I was beautiful to *him*.

"I want to be naked with you," I told him. "Not you or me. I want both of us naked, skin-to-skin, so I can feel you against me."

Adam had his jeans unbuttoned and pushed down instantly.

And I was unable to speak.

He was perfect—hard planes and tight muscles—and every perfect inch was mine for the taking. *For the keeping.* His shoulders and biceps were covered by beautiful tattoos, and his pecs had an older black and gray piece with script.

I swallowed as I studied him.

When I lifted my gaze to look into his eyes, I thought I would incinerate.

He reached down to pull something out of his jeans pocket. He tore open the foil package. "I don't always carry one there," he told me. "I grabbed it before I came into the room."

I nodded, my gaze transfixed by the sight of him rolling the condom over his perfect cock.

We both stepped forward, and then we were skin-to-skin. Finally. I'd spent over a year fantasizing about him, months trying to resist him, weeks trying to forget the taste of him, and hours fearing I'd never feel his touch again.

"And are you mine, Sasha?" His hands slid to my hips, and his fingers curled possessively around me. "Only mine?"

"I am."

"It's about time," he whispered before his mouth crashed down on mine, and he made me forget everything but him.

By the time we made it into the shower, I was trembling from the first orgasm of the day. He smiled affectionately as I leaned against him while he adjusted the water temperature.

We stepped into the water, and he began washing my body with the sort of care he'd used when he'd gone down on me on the sofa.

"No one's ever been like this," I confessed.

He paused in his ministrations. "Like . . .?"

"Gentle, I guess."

He kissed and licked his way across my collarbone, worshipped my breasts until I believed that I could come from that alone, and trailed his fingers over my hips and belly.

"They were fools then," he murmured.

I was torn between wanting to lean back on the wall for support and pressing closer to him. His teeth-tongue-hands-cock were all driving me towards euphoria. "If I die here, it'd be worth it."

He laughed, a beautiful sound full of promise. Then he lifted me up in a sudden motion. Holding me with only one arm, he reached between us and guided himself into me. I felt like my eyes would roll back in sheer bliss.

I moaned as I twined my arms around his neck. The shower wall was cool and slick, and Adam was hard and hot. He didn't move hardly at all for several moments, and there was nothing I could do.

He kissed his way up my throat and to my ear. "I need you," he whispered.

I was pinned to the wall with the strongest man I've ever known pressed into my body. I might not be able to *move*, but I wasn't going to let him have all of the control. I squeezed him, tightening my inner muscles.

He groaned and said, "Perfect. You're perfect."

Then he began to move, so slowly that I felt like every promise of forever that I'd dreamed of was worth giving up if this was all he wanted of me. I'd take it. I'd take whatever terms he needed as long as we had this.

But Adam made my already blissed out mind shatter when he said, "I love you, Sasha. God, I love you so fucking much."

Tears filled my eyes, and I admitted, "Need . . . you . . ."

My admission made him move a little faster, not rough or hurried but that little bit of extra speed that made me go over the edge. "Love you," I gasped as I climaxed around him.

He came with a growl, and for a moment, we were still and shaking.

After several moments when the only sounds were breathing and water crashing, Adam reached out and turned off the water. The sudden silence seemed intimidating.

I lower my legs and stepped back slightly.

Adam lifted his head and met my eyes. "Did you mean it?"

"I did. I tried not to . . . I really tried. I tried to be with . . ." My words stalled. It felt wrong to say another man's name right now.

"Tommy," Adam finished quietly, handing me a towel that I wrapped half-heartedly around me.

I nodded. "I tried. I didn't want to love you. I'm a mess and you—"

"Love you," he interrupted. "I love you. I loved you when you were a mess, and I love you now that you're changing the parts of you that were hurting. I love you either way, but I'm proud of you for the changes you've made."

Carefully, he wrapped both arms around me and carried me from the shower to the bed. When he lowered me to the bed, I had a fleeting thought about the fact that we were soaking wet and about to crawl onto my dry sheets, but then Adam peeled my towel off and dropped it onto the bed.

He pulled me into his arms as we stretched out on the bed, still wet. I shivered slightly, and he pulled the sheet and blanket over us. "I don't want you to think you have to pretend Tommy wasn't in your life. I know he was. I know you cared about him."

"Not like he wanted," I admitted. "I tried. I really did. It wasn't him I dreamed about though."

"You don't have to say anything you don't mean," Adam said in a very calm voice. "I'll love you even if you aren't ready—"

"I'm not saying anything but the truth." I lifted my head and turned so I could look into his eyes. "I've been in denial for a while. Mila says that we both were."

"Mila? From Rio Verde?"

"I called her," I said in a small voice.

He groaned. "Sash!"

"And the shop, yours not the Cave," I added meekly.

He squeezed me to him tightly. "Okay. It's okay. You trust her, and it was just a couple people from there, right?"

I nodded. "I needed to talk about us . . . and someone from Sinners left a message . . . and I was scared and alone, and"—I lower my head back to his chest—"it was stupid. I'm sorry."

Adam didn't tell me I was wrong or that it wasn't a bad idea, all he said was, "We'll sort it out. *Together*. Whatever comes next, we'll sort it out together, Sasha. From here on out, that's the way it's going to be. You and me. We'll figure it out."

"I love you," I said with a happy sigh as I nestled into his arms.

"Say it again," he asked.

I rolled over on top of him and said, "I love you."

The sheet slid down my back, and he stared up at me with that same look of intense desire I'd already started to recognize. "You don't know how long I've wanted to hear that."

"I . . ."—I leaned down and kissed him—"love"—I stilled as he caught one of my nipples in his mouth—"you."

His fingers were inside me, and he nudged my thighs further apart. I kneeled over his hips as he played with my already sensitive body, telling me over and over that he loved me, wanted me, needed me. I came again as he told me I was beautiful, brave, and smart. He slid inside me again as he promised we would start a future together.

And I rode him until we were both unable to say anything else.

ADAM

The next week was perfect. Adam was fairly sure it was the happiest he'd been in his life. And maybe being happy made him careless.

Adam thought that everything was in order. For the first time in his life, he had everything he could want, everything he had wanted. He'd admitted to himself that he loved Sasha last year, but she was still with Tommy then. It made him feel like the worst kind of person, coveting his cousin's girlfriend. He didn't do anything to try to break them up, but he pointed out the truth to both of them when they were on the outs.

That was how he made peace with his feelings. He only reminded them of the facts: the time Tommy was so high that he had his hands on another girl in front of Sasha, the time Sasha was so high she would've agreed to Tommy's suggestion to put on a show in front of everyone in his apartment, the times they fought so loud and long that they were thrown out of bars. There were enough examples of how their relationship was bad for Sasha that it seemed insane that she ever took Tommy back.

But she had. For months, she gave him second chance after

second chance. And Adam could only watch and try to be a friend.

Then there were months when he thought the girl he'd fallen for had been lost under the drugs she and Tommy snorted. Then, she stopped. She stopped being with Tommy, stopped snorting cocaine, stopped destroying her life.

He'd waited for her to take the next step, to *see* him. It didn't happen. He pushed, waited, offered. He'd been on the verge of thinking that she simply wasn't attracted to him. Then, he'd tattooed her. He couldn't mistake the desire in her eyes, not the first time or the third time. He'd broken every ethical code he'd held himself to trying to get her to take that last step toward admitting that they had, at the very least, heat between them.

When she finally did, she ran.

He liked to believe that they'd have still found their way to one another if they hadn't been forced to flee Rio Verde. It didn't actually matter, though. Sasha was finally in his life, and he wasn't going to let anything or anyone take her from him. He was going to protect her and do whatever it took to let her have the future she wanted. If that meant setting down permanent roots, he'd do it. He'd already proven to himself that he was capable of staying in one town for more than a couple of months. He'd done that for her. He'd do whatever else she needed too.

Adam walked into Mezcal Johnny's feeling like the world was sitting in the palm of his hand. He should've known that feeling so good was like a lightning rod for trouble.

That trouble was sitting on one of the four chairs that served as a waiting area for customers. The man was dressed entirely wrong for the end of May in the desert. He had a dark suit, shiny city shoes, and a lying smile. Adam had met dozens of him in the course of his life. They were the men that his Uncle Thomas, Tommy's dad, had called "business associates." The suit stood as the shop door closed behind Adam.

"Adam Bradbery?"

"Yeah."

"I'm a friend of your cousin's," the suit said. "It's a shame what happened to him, but I have some interests of his to pass on to his girlfriend."

"Tommy didn't have a girlfriend," Adam said.

Drunk Dave lifted his head from the catalogue he was perusing. His gaze met Adam's for a moment. In it was a question and an offer of help if necessary.

The suit didn't even acknowledge the older man. That moved him from potential threat to idiotic potential threat in Adam's book. Dave might not be as burly as he'd been in the photos on the shop wall, but he had visible muscles and the sort of hard eyes that said he'd seen things best not discussed.

Adam shook his head once. Dave had a business, a wife, and grandkids to think about. This wasn't his trouble.

"Sasha Kovac," the suit said. "She went by Sugar."

"I knew her back in Rio Verde," Adam allowed. "Maybe you should look there."

"I did." The suit stepped closer. "She left after Tommy's accident."

"He wasn't in an accident. He was shot." Adam tensed.

The man waved his hand dismissively. "Regardless of that, I need to see Sasha."

"She worked at a coffee place there," Adam said. "You could check with them."

He knew he wasn't saying anything the suit didn't already know. This wasn't a casual visit. The suit had assumed that Adam and Sasha had left together.

"I did," the suit said, sliding his suit jacket off and revealing a holstered gun in the process. "I checked with your employer too. I explained that I needed to see you about Thomas' death—"

"Tommy," Adam corrected. "Thomas was my uncle."

The suit nodded and said, "Of course. They said you were working at an old shop, and they kindly helped me with a list of shops where you had done 'guest tattooing.' It took a few days, but I thought it best to come see you as soon as I figured out where you were."

Out of the corner of his eye, Adam could see Dave's hand slip under the counter. There was an alarm there. Alarms meant cops. Cops meant paper trails.

"No," Adam said, turning to Dave.

The distraction was enough to give the suit an opportunity. His fist came at Adam's face, knocking him back slightly. It was the punch of a man used to violence.

But Adam had grown up with violence back in Philadelphia, where he'd been in so many scrapes his mother signed him up for boxing, karate, and every other defense or "anger management" course at the community center—including yoga and guided meditation.

"The first punch was a freebie," Adam said, raising his fists.

"Your cousin stole something my employer would like returned to him," the suit said. "Either you or Miss Kovac have our property."

"I don't know where Sugar is, and I don't have anything."

They exchanged blows for several minutes, and Adam was reluctantly impressed by the man's skill. He fought with enough restraint to make clear that this was not his all. Each punch was a statement, a notice that he was intimidating.

"I'm sorry you lost something, but that doesn't have shit to do with me," Adam said as his fist made contact with the suit's jaw.

The man shook his head slightly, like he had to shake off the hit. "We retrieved the cocaine. All we need is the cash."

"If you've snooped around as much as I think, you know I don't fuck with drugs, and I live simply." Adam didn't take his attention off the suit. "Maybe Tommy got mixed up with someone else."

"But you and Miss Kovac left town," the suit said.

"I identified my cousin's corpse," Adam said coldly. "I was only in town as long as I was because of him. Why would I stay after he was stupid enough to get killed?"

"And your cousin's girlfriend?"

"I saw her around, but I wasn't her best fucking girlfriend or something," Adam scoffed. "She and Tommy had a thing. He'd dead. She's probably holed up at some girl's house weeping or her new guy's place too fucked up to let her tears out."

The suit lowered his fists.

"You know how coked up people are, right?" Adam asked, whispering a silent apology to Sasha for the things he was saying, but that *was* what a lot of people thought: that addicts couldn't recover. Adam knew better, but if it meant this guy took off, Adam would tell him whatever lie he could sell.

It was obvious, too, that the idiot believed Adam. Whether it was because of the way Adam had lived or his well-known disapproval of drugs or some other reason, it didn't matter. The suit accepted Adam's lies.

"You tell me of you hear from her."

"Sure, man. Whatever." Adam held up his hands. "I don't need any trouble."

He took the man's card, and a few minutes later, the suit left.

The door fell closed, and Dave looked at Adam. "I can call my buddy Eli over at the garage. They'll delay the boy's car long enough for you to get to her without him following you once he starts thinking it through a bit more."

Adam nodded. "Do you think he already knows where I'm staying?"

"Doubt it. Hector's about ten seconds from a conspiracy nut. Why else did you think I had to vouch for you to get him to rent you the house? The man's straight-up paranoid. He doesn't even tell himself half of what he knows. That one"—Dave nodded toward the door the suit had exited through—"wouldn't get anything other than nonsense out of Hector."

Adam felt a little terror recede. "How fast can Eli help?"

Dave didn't answer; he just picked up the phone and made arrangements. When he hung up, he said, "Give him twenty, maybe thirty minutes tops, and then you go get her and get out of town."

SASHA

I curled into the bed thinking about Adam instead of napping like I needed to be doing. Even the thought of him made me lose sleep. Being with Adam was different. With him, I felt like I was . . . special. I suspect that had been happening for months. In Adam's eyes, I was strong and brave. I wanted to be that way, to be the girl he saw when he looked at me. When I talked, he listened. When I was nervous, he asked questions.

Of course, I also believed him when he said anything. In the past, he'd reminded me of how much I'd overcome. He'd encouraged me for well over a year. So now—when he said he loved me —I believed him. I trusted Adam as I'd never trusted anyone in my life.

And I'd do whatever it took to stay with him. It felt crazy that after all this time trying to stay away from him, he was mine. He wanted to be with me because of me, of us, not out of duty.

He had a short shift at the shop today, and then we were going to spend the rest of the day together. I wasn't sure what we were doing, but at the end, it didn't matter. I was with him. The rest was just details.

We'll figure them out together.

When I heard the Harley pull up, I had just started drifting off to sleep. Either Dave sent him home early or I'd fallen asleep and not realized it. I hopped out of bed, paused to run my hands through my hair to try and make it look presentable, and then I started toward the door, but it slammed open before I reached it.

"Adam?" I gasped. His shirt was torn, and a bruise was forming on his cheek.

"Pack up."

"What happened?"

"The reason Sinners was trying to reach me was a guy claiming to be my cousin, mine and Tommy's actually." Adam's expression grew darker. "Claimed he was in town to check on me after Tommy's death. Lying fucker. They thought he was honest, though, and so they told him where to look for me."

"I'm so *so* sorry," I started. "It was because of my message, wasn't it?"

"He was already on the way, checking places I'd worked." Adam glanced outside, and I wondered if he was expecting to be followed. "No calls home, though, Sash. We can't talk to anyone there until this shit is resolved. . . *if* it ever gets resolved."

I nodded. Adam was hurt because of me, because I called and left a message at the tattoo shop in Rio Verde. "I screwed up. I shouldn't have called them."

He sighed, pulled me to him and hugged me so tightly that I thought I was going to have to hold my breath for a moment. "I shouldn't have walked out and gotten drunk either. I shouldn't have come to a shop where I used to work. They'd have looked at the shops I'd been at sooner or later."

We stood in a tight embrace for another minute.

"I was terrified that they'd found out where I was staying and come here too. He said he was alone, but I don't know if he was lying." Adam let go of me then. "We need to pack and get gone. Leave the groceries."

"How long?"

"I'm going to hook up the bike trailer, load the Harley, and grab the things we stored in the garage. When that's done, we're on the move."

It didn't take long at all to gather up the bits of things I'd left scattered around the house. Aside from a shirt still draped over the arm of the sofa, I'd put everything away already. I scooped everything out the drawers, dumped it into suitcases, and did a quick check under the bed and throughout the three rooms of the house.

Glancing down, I realized that my clothes were entangled with some of Adam's things in my suitcases, and despite everything, that made me smile. I started to carry all of the bags to the side of the truck.

"We didn't have a lot of things to pack. I gathered all of our clothes—clean and dirty—and our toiletries."

"Almost ready," he said.

Since Adam was still packing the Explorer, I snatched up a few grocery bags and shoved what I could of the food into them too. I couldn't stand around waiting and wringing my hands, and if we had time, I could salvage some of the food.

Not even fifteen minutes after he'd arrived, Adam was in the doorway. "We're loaded."

"All that we've left is some of the stuff in the fridge," I said. I held up the bag in my hand. "This and that one on the left can go in the cooler though."

"Leave the key on the table. Drunk Dave is going to tell them we left early."

A couple of minutes later, we'd tossed the few bags into the back, shoved the one with the ice packs and cold goods in the cooler, and were headed further west.

"We're good together," Adam said.

"I thought we figured that out about a week ago."

He flashed me a smile. "In a crisis we do well too. Teamwork or whatever."

"Figured that out in Rio Verde when we overturned Tommy's place," I pointed out. "And before that when I was trying to get clean."

"I like it." He reached over and caught my hand in his. "Whatever we find out there, we can handle it together."

And that was something I'd never really felt before, the way he treated me like someone he could trust and talk to. My parents had always acted like I was the biggest disappointment in the world. I hadn't talked to them in years. My friends were the casual sort, so there were no great secrets or adventures there. Tommy had alternated between deciding I was a possession and treating me like a child who would get into trouble without supervision. Only Adam had treated me like a partner.

"I love you," I told him. "I'm sorry I screwed up—"

He cut me off, saying, "We both did."

I FINALLY GOT my nap as he drove, but I woke when we stopped along the I-5 somewhere a few hours later. The drive from Joshua Tree over to Los Angeles isn't that long, and we thought about staying there. The city is huge, so losing ourselves there would be easy. It would also be expensive . . . and in L.A. A lot of people seemed to love it, but I wasn't a fan of Southern California. It had the sun we had in the desert, but it had smog and noise and traffic. I hated all of those things.

"You dozed through L.A.," Adam said when we stopped. He shook his head. "It's not that late in the day, Sash. How are you even tired?"

I lifted both brows as I stared at him silently for a moment.

"Are you seriously asking that? Did you miss the fact that we've been spending a lot of the last six nights having sex—"

"Making love," he interjected.

"Right, but whether you call it making love or having sex, we've been doing that, and I've worked the breakfast shift the past three days."

"I get up," he said.

"And then drive back to the house and crawl into bed to sleep," I pointed out. "I nap when you work in the afternoon or evening, but today . . . no nap."

"You napped."

"I did," I agreed, looking out at the chain coffee shop where he had stopped. "And I got to miss L.A. because of it. Win, win."

Adam shook his head. "It's not an awful place."

"I've never been to the Pacific Northwest," I reminded him.

"Me either."

"So?"

"We already passed L.A., Sash. Let me get some coffee and stretch, and then we'll keep going." He held out a hand to me, as if I needed help getting out of the Explorer. He did that a lot, chivalrous hand-taking and door opening. It was an oddly sweet gesture he'd made from time to time when we were going some-where, and now that we were an "us," he did it constantly.

He was silent as we went inside and ordered, but he was smil-ing. That smile made everything in my life better. I'd already admitted to myself that I'd do a lot to keep getting those smiles from him, and luckily, he seemed to want to give them all to me.

A little while later, we were on the road again. I didn't know how far we'd drive tonight. I wasn't even sure where we were going.

"Do we have a plan?" I asked finally when we were some-where near a little town called Coalinga. We'd left Joshua Tree about six hours ago, and although I knew California was a big state, it seemed crazy that we were still in it after that many hours of driving.

"Follow the interstate until we decide to stop," Adam said with a shrug.

"In Oregon or Washington?" I asked.

"Unless you want to keep going up into Canada. Vancouver's supposed to be amazing."

I laughed and pointed out, "So are Portland and Seattle. Do you have any preference?"

"Not yet." He reached over and took my hand in his. "Wherever you're safe and in my arms sounds perfect to me. We can pick which city once we're there."

I squeezed his hand. "That works for me."

"I have almost everything I've made the past six years saved up. Once we're sure we're clear all of the trouble back in Rio Verde, I was thinking of opening up a shop of my own, settling down somewhere," he said in a voice that was lighter than his words. "For now, though, we could just travel. You said you wanted to do that."

"I love you," I said.

He lifted my hand to his lips and kissed my knuckles. "I love you too, Sash."

"So can we stop at a hotel for the night, get a room for you, me, and the Harley?" I said, remembering what he'd told me last month about keeping his bike in the house with us.

He grinned. "Definitely."

All I'd wanted was a good man, a little house, and some travel. In the past few weeks, I'd found two of them, and once we were able to settle down somewhere, I knew I could have the third one, too. I wasn't sure how or when, but even though we were on the run, I was already happier than I'd ever been.

Unruly

Chapter 1

A lamo stood in the middle of a sea of boxes that filled his new house. He was no stranger to moving. Growing up, he'd been rousted from his bed more times than he could count to move to a new place in the middle of the night. His mother would let the back rent build up as far as she could, and then they'd skip out. Mix in a few turns in foster care over the years when she was arrested, and he'd become something of a pro at traveling light and moving quickly. This time, though, he was moving everything he'd accumulated over several years of stability. He had absolutely no desire to put it to rights in a new place.

Truth be told, this new house was the nicest place he'd ever lived. It wasn't *home*, though. Home was a modest-sized apartment in Durham, North Carolina. Home was having his sister Zoe in the house, badly imitating his Spanish cusswords and singing like a cat in a surly mood—and he missed it.

He'd lost that right when he'd lost his temper. He knew it, but that didn't make it any less frustrating. He'd done the right thing, and there wasn't a minute of it that he regretted. The man deserved every punch, but that was neither here nor there. Truth didn't change facts, and the facts were that Alamo was a big man, and his long-gone father wasn't as white as his mama had been. Race shouldn't matter, but sometimes having darker skin still did, especially in a city where drug traffic was as common as it was in Durham. The police tended to blame it on one segment of the population, those with darker skin. He was a large man with darker skin. To add to that, once the police saw the motorcycle club patches on his jacket, Alamo was far too likely to end up in jail if he stayed in North Carolina.

This time they had a reason of sorts. He had put that *pendejo* in the hospital. And an uptown white boy in his expensive clothes could afford the sort of lawyers who twisted truth until it looked nothing like reality. Alamo knew it, had known it before he'd taken the first swing. Sometimes, though, a man had to stand up for a woman regardless of the cost. Zoe's friend had no one else to stand up for her, so Alamo did what needed doing. It was that simple.

"You can't just do that!" Zoe snapped at him when he'd walked into the little apartment they shared. "I might not be a kid, but I still don't need my brother in the lockup."

"He hurt Ana."

"You are not the law, Alejandro. You wear that jacket"—she pointed at the vest with the Southern Wolves patches prominently displayed—"and you forget that you're not above the law."

"Lobita," he started.

"Don't you 'little wolf' me, mister!" His sister's hands landed on their

customary position on her hips. She was a tiny little thing, but she had the attitude of a dozen girls. "If you end up in jail, I'll . . . I'll find someone big enough to kick your ass. Then where will you be, eh?"

Alamo bowed his head, as much to hide his smile as to let her know he was listening to her chastisement.

"You call Nicky, you hear me? You find out where you can move because you're not staying here. That boy . . . he has friends. I don't want this to get worse."

"Lobita . . ."

"No! You call your Wolves, and you move. We talked about it for next year, anyhow. Clean start." Zoe took a shaky breath, let it out, and looked at him. "Ana says thank you and that she's okay. She's . . . sorry."

"Don't need to be sorry. She did nothing wrong, Zoe. You make sure she gets that." His hands fisted despite his intention to keep calm, and the already bloodied knuckles smarted.

Alamo might not have had a father most of his life, but he knew what a man was supposed to be like just the same. Growing up, he'd just studied what his mother's long list of lovers did. Whatever they did, he did the opposite. That was all the guidance he'd needed. That was why Alamo went after the buttoned-up man-boy who'd gotten Ana drunk and taken what wasn't his right to take.

"Call Nicky," Zoe said, and then she turned away. "And put oint-ment on those cuts."

She was right. Being the stand-in parent for Zoe had always been harder because she *was* right more often than not. Her excesses of common sense made her awfully hard to handle. Of course it also meant that it was less worrisome to leave her behind with Ana. She'd be okay; he knew that. Both of the Díaz siblings were survivors.

So far there hadn't been any charges filed, and the jackass who hurt Ana claimed never to have seen Alamo's face. He *did* see Alamo's jacket, though, and it was best for everyone if there was no reason for the police to be looking too closely at the Wolves.

The local chapter president, Nicky, agreed with Zoe, so he'd made a call to another chapter. Within forty-eight hours, Alamo's things had been boxed, and he was in Tennessee. Between a move and a stay in jail, moving was a better choice—but that still didn't mean Alamo was happy with it.

He looked around the cluttered house. Boxes and furniture sat in a jumble, but he needed to get out. Being here, being alone with his thoughts, wasn't going to do anything but make him think about the mess he'd gotten mixed up in. He didn't regret it. He didn't think he was wrong to defend Ana. That didn't mean the consequences were easy to take.

He walked outside, pulled the door shut behind him, and headed to the bar that the Tennessee chapter frequented. Getting to know his new brothers was the best thing he could do now. The Southern Wolves were the only family he had other than Zoe, and while Zoe would visit, she was still in North Carolina while she finished up her college degree.

By the time he pulled his Harley into the parking lot of Whiskey & Wolves, he felt more like himself. All he needed was to stay focused. No distractions. No trouble. No fights unless they were ordered by the club. He had to focus on his job, the Wolves, and not let himself get invested in anyone else's life. He could keep his distance from everyone. That was the one surefire way to keep his temper under control.

No more bad habits. No more mistakes—regardless of how good the reason for them was. Tennessee was going to be the beginning of a new lifestyle, one that would keep him out of trouble and able to build a stable home for his sister once she finished college.

~

"Ellie?" Noah reached out, fingers catching a lock of hair and tugging like we were the kids we hadn't been in years. Noah was turning twenty-four this year, old enough to have more of a plan for his life, old enough to stop running from anything that had even the shadow of commitment to it.

I was only two years younger than him, but sometimes I felt older. He was a mistake I kept making and had been making since not long after I was old enough to get a driver's license. Noah helped me learn, and we'd celebrated with what had turned into a decidedly unhealthy relationship. I wasn't ever going to get my life together if I didn't figure out how to change my bad habits, and Noah Dash was a bad habit. We were never going to be anything but friends who were naked together sometimes.

He was propped up on one arm in his bed, looking like we'd been doing exactly what we had been.

"Do you want a ride to the bar tonight?"

"I thought you didn't want me on your bike where we might be seen," I asked, my voice sounding a little more upset than I wanted to admit. He'd given me a lift to his apartment, but that wasn't quite the same.

"What's between us is between *us*," he said, as if that answer was going to sound less irritating with repetition. It didn't.

I rolled onto my side so I was facing him. "I'm going to drive myself."

"Come on, Ellie, don't be like that."

"Leave it alone." I folded my arms, feeling silly as I did so. It was hard to look stern while we were both naked.

"You know people would misunderstand if you were on my bike regularly." Noah's fingers trailed up my spine. "Showing up at Wolves is like a statement."

"Well, we wouldn't want them to *misunderstand*."

"There's no one else on the bike." Noah sat up and eased closer. "You know that, don't you? I might go on a date or whatever, but that's not anything. I just like a little strange, you know?"

"I know, Noah." I'd known that he wasn't particularly *celibate* before we were together, and that hadn't ever changed. It was his way of making quite clear that he wasn't in a relationship.

I wasn't sure whether I was more embarrassed that I'd wasted years in and out of Noah's bed or that I'd resorted to manipulation to try to get him to see that we *were* having a relationship. Either way, the truth of the matter was that Noah Dash wasn't going to change—and neither was I. I didn't want forever, but I was over being someone's secret. He wouldn't carry me on his Harley more than once in a while because people might think I mattered. God forbid, they might even think I was his old lady. The truth was that I was his best friend and regular bedmate since we were young enough to start exploring. That was it, though.

I used to think it was enough.

I used to think it would change, that he would change.

I even used to think *I* might change.

"Do you think you'll ever let people know about us?" I asked, even now hoping that he'd tell me I was wrong, even now hoping that there was an answer he could offer that would let us keep this messed-up thing that we'd had. Neither one of us had ever tried dating anyone else. We'd settled for this, and it was no good. Not for me. Not for him.

"What if people *did* know?" I asked, pushing a little harder for the answer I hoped to hear.

Instead he looked as if I'd just told him I loved him. Sheer terror was written on his face. "Ellie . . . come on. People know we're friends. All they don't know is that we do *this*." He gestured between us at the bed. "Why would we need to tell anyone our business?"

That's all this was to him: friends who sometimes had sex.

That was the bald truth. We were friends, so we talked, and if we were in a bad way about anything, we knew that we could call at any hour of the day or night. And if we had a need for something other than talk, we had that too. It looked a lot like a relationship, and maybe it was. It wasn't one that worked for me, though. I wasn't ready for kids or a husband or any of that forever stuff, but I was ready to *matter*. I was ready not to be a dirty secret.

And I was ready for someone who *knew* why I was in a lousy mood this week, who cared enough to remember what week it was, who understood why I needed reassurance. I didn't want to have to tell Noah to be kind to me because I needed it a little extra *this week*.

Noah wouldn't change, and I couldn't. What we had wasn't enough. I was done with that, with *him*, with being the girl who didn't deserve more.

I started to climb out of bed to grab my clothes.

"Where are *you* going?" Noah tugged me back onto the bed and rolled me under him. "I just got you here, El."

"You got me here six years ago, Noah."

"I did, didn't I?" He grinned down at me. "Beautiful Miss Ellen, all naked and in my sheets . . . so why can't I take you to the bar tonight? It's been a while. No one would think anything."

"Just let it go. Please?" I asked, hating that he thought that my worry was being found out. I'd all but asked him to be open about us, and he still couldn't hear what I was telling him.

"I'll take you home later if you still want to get your car." He was curled behind me, holding me to him as he did only when he was too exhausted to remember that friends don't cuddle. He kissed my shoulder and murmured, "I hate when we fight, Ellie. Just think about it."

And then he slept . . . and I slid out of his bed for the last time. I felt like a thief as I tiptoed over to gather my clothes, shoes, and books—but better a thief than a fool. Maybe there wasn't anyone out there who would be happy to be with me. Maybe I was an idiot for caring that Noah didn't want more. I didn't mean to care, but I had enough of my heart in the mix that I couldn't stay, not if I wanted to respect myself at all. The next time I let a man into my bed, he sure as hell wasn't getting into my heart. Keeping sex and love in separate rooms was a safer plan. I didn't love Noah anymore, but I had been lingering on the edge of it far too long. I could love him like a friend, but I couldn't do it *and* sleep with him. I'd rather have love *or* sex because this half-assed mess of neither and both was breaking my heart. No matter what, though, I wouldn't be hidden away by anyone again.

"Never again," I promised myself as I went downstairs.

At the bottom of the steps, I pulled the building door closed behind me. Not for the first time, I was left stranded because of Noah Dash.

Truthfully, I was stranded in more ways than one. Job opportunities meant moving, and because of Noah I hadn't been willing to leave Williamsville. Admittedly, fashion industry jobs weren't thick on the vine in Tennessee—but those that *were* certainly weren't in Williamsville. I was here because of him, though.

My more immediate issue was getting out of his neighborhood. Later when I was calm, I could think about getting out of town entirely . . . or decide if I really wanted to go. For now I needed a ride.

I could call my mother—who was more of a roommate than a parent—but I didn't know that I was in the mood for her counseling me on patience. For reasons I wouldn't even try to fathom, she thought Noah could do no wrong. That left me with calling my friends who didn't know about Noah, calling Noah's cousin, Killer, or calling the bar.

I called the bar.

"What's up, little bit?" Mike asked.

"I need a ride. No questions, and no one who'd tell tales about . . . anything." I walked farther from the building where Noah lived. I felt like a vagabond with my boots, bag, and helmet, but I was afraid I'd wake Noah if I tried to put them on inside.

Mike sighed. "I can call a taxicab. Depending on who's working, they might not tell Miss Bitty."

"Ugh." I sat on the curb and shoved my feet into my boots. "Mama's got everyone in her damn pocket. I swear she'd put a tracking chip in my ass if the veterinarian would do it."

Mike snorted. "Don't go giving her ideas."

It was one of the mysteries of my life. My mother never put any restrictions on me, but she kept awfully close tabs on my comings and goings. There was no way that the local drivers wouldn't tell her where I was.

"I can send the new guy to fetch you," Mike said. "He just walked in. Seems a good sort. Wouldn't tell . . . either of the young'uns."

"That works."

Mike paused and cleared his throat before asking, "Do I need to guess where you are, or do I just assume you're *with* one of the young'uns?"

"Got it in one." That was the thing. People *did* know, maybe not everything, but enough for me to be embarrassed by the fact that Noah treated me like I was a secret.

"Do I need to send a helmet?"

"I have mine," I said, glancing at it, trying not to think of going shopping for it with Noah and Killer. "I just need a ride . . . and if you can avoid mentioning it to Uncle Karl or Echo."

Mike's tone shifted. "You know better than that, Ellen."

I nodded even though he couldn't see me. Everything to do with Noah or Killer was reported to the Wolves' president *and* to the biker who'd raised both boys. It was simply the way of it. Hell, I'd been the one reporting things over the years. Everyone did it.

Echo cared about every little detail of their lives. Nothing was considered too insignificant to mention. Killer had coped by devoting himself to Echo, becoming Echo's right hand. Noah had done the opposite—refusing to even be patched into the Wolves.

"What's the new guy's name?" I asked.

"Alamo."

"Okay." Admittedly this was a somewhat silly question. I'd know him when he arrived because he would be wearing club colors, the Wolves' insignia clearly marked on either a black leather vest or jacket. Plus, there weren't any Wolves I didn't know *other* than the new guy, so a biker who arrived with club colors was obviously my ride. That said, I wasn't going to be rude and not know his name.

I disconnected and sat on the curb. I wondered if anyone else realized that this week was the anniversary of my father's death. Noah certainly hadn't, and that told me more than anything else. A man who wasn't there for me wasn't what I needed. A woman didn't *need* a man at all. Mama had been telling me that since my father died . . . but sometimes I wanted one, not just in my sheets but in my life. I wanted someone who cared about me, who remembered to hold me, who treated me like I was special. Instead, I was waiting for a stranger.

The Wicked & The Dead is AVAILABLE NOW!

"I loved *The Wicked and The Dead*! A sassy, ass-kicking heroine, a deliciously mysterious fae hero, and a wonderful mix of action and romance. Add that to Melissa's usual great world-building, and I'm already looking forward to book 2!"
— Jeaniene Frost, *NYT* Bestselling Author

Geneviève Crowe makes her living beheading the dead. But now, her magic has gone sideways, and the only person strong enough to help her is the one man who could tempt her to think about picket fences: Eli Stonecroft, a faery bar-owner in New Orleans.

When human businessmen start turning up as *draugr*, the queen of the again-walkers and the wealthy son of one of the victims, both hire Geneviève to figure it out. She works to keep her magic in check, the dead from crawling out of their graves, and enough money for a future that might be a lot longer than she'd like. Neither her heart nor her life are safe now that she's juggling a faery, murder, and magic.

Chapter One

Autumn in the South was still both humid and hot. New Orleans was always a wet city. Wet air. Wet drizzle. Beer soaked streets. *Other* things spilling out from behind trash bins. Sometimes, the heavy air and frequent rain was just this side of too much.

Most nights, there was nowhere else I'd rather be. We were a city risen from the ashes, over and over. Plagues, floods, monsters. New Orleans didn't stop, didn't give up, and I was proud of that. Tonight, though, I watched the fog roll out like a cheap film effect, and a good book in front of a warm fire sounded far better than work. The nonstop rain this month would wash away evidence of the things that happened in New Orleans' darkened corners, but I could prevent bloodshed. It was more or less what I did. Sometimes, I spilled a bit of blood, but if we weighed it all out, I was fairly sure I was one of the good guys.

More curves and sass than actual *guys*, but the point held. White hat. Dingy around the edges. I blame my persistent nagging guilt.

A *thump* on the other side of the wall made me pause.

Could I hurl myself over the wall into Cypress Grove Cemetery? It wasn't the *worst* idea ever—or even this month—which said more about my life than I'd like to admit.

I listened for more sounds. *Nothing*. No scrabbling. No growling.

I needed to be on the other side of the wall where tombs were lined up like miniature houses. The tree branches I'd used last time were gone, probably trimmed by someone who saw their potential. Now, there was no graceful way to hurl myself over the ten-foot wall.

Every cemetery in the nation now had taller walls and plenty of newly-opened space for the dead. Cemeteries had become "stage one" of the verification of death process. Honestly, I guess graves were better than cold storage at the morgue. The lack of heartbeat made it impossible to know if the corpses would walk-again, and those of us who advocated for beheading all corpses were deemed callous.

I wasn't sure I was callous for wanting the dead to stay dead. I knew what they were capable of before the world at large did.

At least I was prepared. A moment or so later, I shoved a metal spike into the wall, cutting my palm in the process.

"Shit. Damn. Monkey balls."

A ripple of light flashed around me the moment my blood dripped to the soil. At least the light was magic, not the police or a tourist with a camera. While the laws were ever-changing, B&E was still illegal. And I was breaking into a cemetery where I might need to carry out a contracted beheading. *That* was illegal, too.

It simply wasn't a photo-ready moment—although with my long dyed-blue hair and nearly translucent skin, I was far too photogenic. I won't say I look like I've been drained of both blood and color, but I will admit that next to a lot of the folks in my city, I look like I've been bleached.

I fumbled with my gloves, trapping my blood inside the thick leather before I resumed shoving climbing cams into gaps in the wall. Normally, cams held the ropes that climbers use. Tonight, they'd be like tiny foot supports. If I were human, this wouldn't work out well.

I'm not.

Mostly, I'd say I am a witch, but that is the polite truth. I am more like witch-with-hard-to-explain-extras. That smidge of blood I'd spilled was enough to send out "wakey, wakey" messages to whatever corpses were listening, but the last time I'd had to bleed for them to rest again, I'd needed to shed more than a cup of blood.

I concentrated on not sending out a second magic flare and continued to insert the cams.

Rest. Stay. I felt silly thinking messages to the dead, but better silly than planning for excess bleeding.

At least this job *should* be an easy one. My task was to find out if Alice Navarro was again-walking or if she was securely in her vault. I hoped for the latter. Most people hired me to ease their dearly departed back in the "departed" category, but the Navarro family was the other sort. They missed her, and sometimes grief makes people do things that are on the wrong side of rational.

My pistol had tranquilizer rounds tonight. If Navarro was awake, I'd need to tranq her. If she wasn't, I could call it a night—unless there were other again-walkers. That's where the beheading came in. Straight-forward. Despite the cold and wet, I still hoped for the best. All things considered, I really was an optimist at heart.

At the top of the wall, I swung my leg over the stylish spikes cemented there and dropped into the wet grass. I was braced for it, but when I landed, it wasn't dew or rain that made me land on my ass.

An older man, judging by the tufts of grey hair on the bloodied body, in a security guard uniform had bled out on the ground. Something--most likely an again-walker--had gnawed on the security guard's face. Who had made the decision to have a living man with no special skills stand inside the walls of a cemetery? Now, he was dead.

I whispered a quick prayer before surveying my surroundings. Once I located the *draugr*, I could call in the location of the dead man. First, though, I had to find the face-gnawer who killed him. Since my magic was erratic, I didn't want to send a voluntary pulse out to find my prey. That would wake the truly dead, and there were plenty of them here to wake.

Several rows into the cemetery, I found Alice Navarro's undisturbed grave. No upheaval. No turned soil. Mrs. Navarro was well and truly dead. My clients had their answer—but now, I had a mystery. Which cemetery resident had killed the security guard?

A sound drew my attention. A thin hooded figure, masked like they were off to an early carnival party, stared back at me. They didn't move like they were dead. Too slow. Too human. And *draugr* weren't big on masks.

"Hey!" My voice seemed too loud. "You. What are you . . ."

The figure ran, and several other voices suddenly rang out. Young voices. Teens inside the cemetery.

"Shit cookies!" I ran after the masked person. Who in the name of all reason would be in among the graves at night? I ran through the rows of graves, looking for evidence of waking as I went.

"Bitch!"

The masked figure was climbing over the wall with a ladder, the chain sort you use in home fire-emergencies. Two teens tried to grab the person. One kid was kneeling, hand gripping his shoulder in obvious pain.

And there, several feet away, was Marie and Edward Chevalier's grave. The soil was disturbed, as if a pack of excited dogs had been digging. The person in the mask was not the dead one in the nearby grave. There *was* a recently dead *draugr*.

And kids.

I glanced back at the teens.

A masked stranger, a dead security guard, a *draugr*, and kids. This was a terrible combination.

The masked person dropped something and pulled a gun. The kids backed away quickly, and the masked person glanced at me before scrambling the rest of the way over the wall—all while awkwardly holding a gun.

"Are you okay?" I asked the kids, even as my gaze was scanning for the *draugr*.

"She stabbed Gerry," the girl said, pointing at the kid on the ground.

The tallest of the teens grabbed the thing the intruder dropped and held it up. A syringe.

"She?" I asked.

"Lady chest," the tall one explained. "When I ran into her, I felt her—"

"Got it." I nodded, glad the intruder with the needle was gone, but a quick glance at the stone by the disturbed grave told me that a fresh body had been planted there two days ago. That was the likely cause of the security guard's missing face. I read the dates on the stone: Edward was not yet dead. Marie was.

I was seeking Marie Chevalier.

"Marie?" I whispered loudly as the kids talked among themselves. The last thing I needed right now was a *draugr* arriving to gnaw on the three dumb kids. "Oh, Miss Marie? Where are you?"

Marie wouldn't answer, even if she had been a polite Southern lady. *Draugr* were like big infants for the first decade and change: they ate, yelled, and stumbled around.

"There's a real one?" the girl asked.

I glanced at the kids. I was calling out a thing that would *eat* them if they had been alone with it, and they seemed excited. Best case was a drooling open-mouthed lurch in my direction. Worst case was they all died.

"Go home," I said.

Instead they trailed behind me as I walked around, looking for Marie. I passed by the front gate—which was now standing wide open.

"Did you do that?" The lock had been removed. The pieces were on the ground. Cut through. Marie was not in the cemetery.

Shaking heads. "No, man. The ladder the bitch used was ours."

Intruder. With a needle. Possibly also the person who left the gate open? Had someone wanted Marie Chevalier released? Or was that a coincidence? Either way, a face-gnawer was loose somewhere in the city, one of the who-knows-how-many *draugr* that hid here or in the nearby suburbs or small towns.

I pushed the gates closed and called it in to the police. "Broken gate at Cypress Grove. Cut in pieces."

"Miss Crowe," the woman on dispatch replied. "Are you injured?"

"No. The *lock* was cut. Bunch of kids here." I shot them a look. "Said it wasn't them."

"I will send a car," she said. A longer than normal pause. "Why are *you* there, Miss Crowe?"

I smothered a sigh. It complicated my life that so many of the cops recognized me, that dispatch did, that the ER folks at the hospital did. It wasn't like New Orleans was *that* small.

"Do you log my number?" I asked. "Or is it my voice?"

Another sigh. Another pause. She ignored my questions. "Details?"

"I was checking on a grave here. It's intact, but the cemetery gate's busted," I explained.

"I noted that," she said mildly. "Are the kids alive?"

"Yeah. A person in a mask tried to inject one of them, and a guard inside is missing a lot of his face. No *draugr* here now, but the grave of Marie and Edward Chevalier is broken out. I'm guessing it was her that killed the guard."

The calm tone was gone. "There's a car about two blocks away. You and the children—"

"I'm good." I interrupted. "Marie's long gone, I guess. I'll be sure the kids are secure, but—"

"Miss Crowe! You don't know if she's still there or nearby. You need to be relocated to safety, too."

"Honest to Pete, you all need to worry a lot less about me," I said.

She made a noise that reminded me of my mother. Mama Lauren could fit a whole lecture in one of those "uh-huh" noises of hers. The woman on dispatch tonight came near to matching my mother.

"Someone *cut* the lock," I told dispatch. "What we need to know is why. And who. And if there are other opened cemeteries." I paused. "And who tried to inject the kid."

I looked at them. They were in a small huddle. One of them dropped and stomped the needle. I winced. That was going to make investigating a lot harder.

Not my problem, I reminded myself. I was a hired killer, not a cop, not a detective, not a nanny.

"Kid probably ought to get a tox screen and tetanus shot," I muttered.

Dispatch made an agreeing noise, and said, "Please try not to 'find' more trouble tonight, Miss Crowe."

I made no promises.

When I disconnected, I looked at the kids. "Gerry, right?"

The kid in the middle nodded. White boy. Looking almost as pale as me currently. I was guessing he was terrified.

"Let me see your arm."

He pulled his shirt off. It looked like the skin was torn.

"Do not scream," I said. My eyes shifted into larger versions of a snake's eyes. I knew what it looked like, and maybe a part of me was okay with letting them see because nobody would believe them if they did tell. They were kids, and while a lot had changed in the world, people still doubted kids when they talked.

More practically, though, as my eyes changed I could see in a way humans couldn't.

Green. Glowing like a cheap neon light. The syringe had venom. *Draugr* venom. It wasn't inside the skin. The syringe was either jammed or the kid jerked away.

"Water?"

One of the kids pulled a bottle from his bag, and I washed the wound. "Don't touch the fucking syringe." I pointed at it. "Who stomped on it? Hold your boot up."

I rinsed that, too. Venom wasn't the sort of thing anyone wanted on their skin unless they wanted acid-burn.

"Venom," I said. "That was venom in the needle. You could've died. And"—I pointed behind me—"there was a *draugr* here. Guy got his face chewed off."

They were listening, seeming to at least. I wasn't their family, though. I was a blue-haired woman with some weapons and weird eyes. The best I could do was hand them over to the police and hope they weren't stupid enough to end up in danger again tomorrow.

New Orleans had more than Marie hiding in the shadows. *Draugr* were fast, strong, and difficult to kill. If not for their need to feed on the living like mindless beasts the first few decades after resurrection, I might accept them as the next evolutionary step. But I wasn't a fan of anything—mindless or sentient—that stole blood and life.

Marie might have been an angel in life, but right now she was a killer.

In my city.

If I found the person or people who decided to release Marie —or the woman with the syringe--I'd call the police. I tried to avoid killing the living. But if I found Marie, or others like her, I wasn't calling dispatch. When it came to venomous killers, I tended to be more of a behead first, ask later kind of woman.

ABOUT THE AUTHOR

Ronnie Douglas was the pseudonym for Melissa Marr's romance novels. It is *such* a secret that the first Ronnie book HarperCollins printed lists Melissa as the copyright holder & lists her email for info on Ronnie.

So far Melissa Marr's books have been translated into twenty-eight languages and been bestsellers internationally as well as domestically (NY Times, Los Angeles Times, USA Today, and Wall Street Journal). Accolades include Good Morning America Summer Pick, Scottish Book Trust, Red Maple finalist (in both Ontario and Manitoba), and Goodreads Good Choice Award and RWA RITA award. She is best known for the Wicked Lovely series for teens, the *Graveminder* for adults, and her picturebook *Bunny Roo, I Love You.* She currently lives with her family in Arizona.

Signed Copies:

To order signed copies of my books (with free ebook included in some cases), go to MelissaMarrBooks.com

Adult Thriller

Pretty Broken Things (2020; psychological thriller)

Adult Fantasy

Graveminder (HarperCollins, 2011)

The Arrivals (HarperCollins, 2012)

Cold Iron Heart (2020; *Wicked Lovely* adult)

The Wicked & The Dead (2020; Urban Fantasy)

The Kiss & The Killer (2021; Urban Fantasy)

Romance Writing as Ronnie Douglas

Undaunted (2015)

Unruly (2016)

Unlawful (2019)

Young Adult

Wicked Lovely series (HarperCollins, 2007-2012)

Made For You (HarperCollins,, 2013)

Seven Black Diamonds (HarperCollins, 2015)

One Blood Ruby (HarperCollins, 2016)

Middle Grade

The Hidden Knife (Penguin, 2021)

Loki's Wolves (with Kelley Armstrong, 2012)

Odin's Ravens (with Kelley Armstrong 2013)

Thor's Serpents (with Kelley Armstrong, 2014)

Collections:

Tales of Folk & Fey (2019)

Dark Court Faery Tales (2019)

This Fond Madness (2017)

Co-Edited with Kelley Armstrong (with HarperTeen)

Enthralled

Shards & Ashes

Co-Edited with Tim Pratt (with Little, Brown)

Rags & Bones

www.ingramcontent.com/pod-product-compliance
Lightning Source LLC
Chambersburg PA
CBHW030633190726
48286CB00008B/2514